Maz Harris

BIKER

Birth of a modern-day outlaw

faber and faber

LONDON · BOSTON

First published in 1985
by Faber and Faber Limited
3 Queen Square London WC1N 3AU

Printed in Great Britain by
Butler & Tanner Ltd, Frome and London

© Maz Harris, 1985

British Library Cataloguing in Publication Data

Harris, Maz
   Bikers: birth of a modern-day outlaw.
   1. Motorcycle gangs—History
   I. Title
   305.5'68   HV6486

   ISBN 0–571–13510–2
Library of Congress Cataloging in Publication Data

Harris, Maz.
   Bikers: birth of a modern-day outlaw.
   1. Motorcycle gangs—Great Britain. 2. Subculture.
   I. Title
   HV6491.G7H37 1985   302.3'4   85–10157

   ISBN 0–571–13510–2 (pbk.)

A minute holds them, who have come to go:
The self-defined astride the created will
They burst away; the towns they travel through
Are home for neither bird nor holiness,
For birds and saints complete their purposes.
At worst, one is in motion; and at best,
Reaching no absolute, in which to rest,
One is always nearer by not keeping still.

Thom Gunn, 'On the Move'

For KONG, *H.A.M.C.K.E.*

CONTENTS

ACKNOWLEDGEMENTS

I've never written a book before, so I don't really know quite where to start (or stop) thanking all the people who actually got this thing off the ground and into print. Just in case I've inadvertently missed anyone out and hurt their feelings – tough.

Having made that clear, I'm nevertheless ever so grateful to the following for their help, encouragement, comments, suggestions and kicks up the arse:

Pete Townshend
Joanna Marston
Ian Mutch
Bob Touchette
Lemmy
Bruce Springsteen
Harry Winch
Dave Taylor
Deborah Davies
John Reed
Stu Garland
Simon Firth
Bob Fine
Peter Fairbrother
Cuf
Kong
The Magic Rat
Herman
Cass
Scrumpy

Dennis
Big John
Squint
Gary
Andy
Shaun
Bryron Bates
Anni Stephens
Steve Myatt
Crazy Horse
Sam Singh
Wolfie
Krazy Ken
Tramp
Bilbo
All my H.A. brothers
My family
All my good friends around the world

Thank you.

M.H.
October 1984

For permission to reprint copyright material we gratefully acknowledge the following:

Faber and Faber Ltd and Farrar, Straus and Giroux, Inc. for an excerpt from 'On the Move' from *Selected Poems 1950–1979* by Thom Gunn, copyright © 1957, 1958, 1979, Thom Gunn; James Fenton for 'The Wild Ones'; Bruce Springsteen for 'The Angel' © Bruce Springsteen, 1972; Carlin Music Corporation, London, England, and Chappell/Intersong Music Group USA for an excerpt from 'Black Denim Trousers and Motorcycle Boots' by The Cheers; written by Jerry Leiber and Mike Stoller; Paisano Publications, Inc. for 'On Seeing The Wild One' by Albert Drake; Tricky Tramp and Lemmy for 'Iron Horse'; M.C.A. Music Australia Pty Ltd for 'Born to be Wild' (Mars/Bonfire) by Steppenwolf, © Music Corporation of America Inc.; CBS Songs Ltd for 'Psycle Sluts' © 1983, from the book *Ten Years in an Open-Necked Shirt* written by John Cooper Clarke, published by Arena Books; and Peter Maurice Music Co. Ltd, London, and ATV Music Corp. for an extract from 'Rip It Up' written by Blackwell/Marascalco, © 1956, Venice Music Inc.

For permission to reproduce the photographs that appear in the book we acknowledge the following with gratitude:

Brent Walker Film Distributors Ltd and Osprey Films Ltd (no. 33 from *Quadrophenia*); Columbia Pictures Industries Inc. (nos. 6, 7, 8 from *The Wild One*; nos. 41 and 42 from *Easy Rider*); *Life* magazine (no. 5 by Barney Peterson); *Los Angeles Times* (nos. 3 and 4 by Barney Peterson); Mainline Pictures (nos. 1 and 22 from *Loveless*); Cliff Marsh (no. 139); Ian Mutch (nos. 34–40, 45, 46, 52, 54–64, 66, 67, 69–72, 74–90, 92, 95, 96, 97, 100, 103, 104, 106–18, 120–6, 129, 131–8); Pat Rooney Productions (no. 51 from *Hells Angels '69*, directed by Lee Madden, Executive Producer, Pat Rooney); Dave Taylor (nos. 2, 13, 23, 24, 26–31); Bob Touchette (nos. 43, 44, 47–50, 53, 65, 68, 73, 91, 93, 94, 98, 99, 101, 102, 105, 119, 127, 128, 130); Harry Winch (nos. 9–12, 14–21, 25, 32).

Faber and Faber would like to apologize for any errors or omissions in either of the above lists.

LIVING THE LIFE ...

Here come the capybaras on their bikes.
They swerve into the friendly, leafy square
Knocking the angwantibos off their trikes,
Giving the old-age coypus a bad scare.
They specialize in nasty, lightning strikes.
They leave the banks and grocers' shops quite bare,
They swagger through the bardoors for a shot
Of anything the barman hasn't got.

They spoil the friendly rodent rodeos
By rustling the grazing flocks of mice.
They wear enormous jackboots on their toes.
Insulted by a comment, in a trice
They whip their switchblades out beneath your nose.
Their favourite food is elephant and rice.
Their personal appearance is revolting.
Their fur is never brushed and always moulting.

And in the evening when the sun goes down
They take the comely women in their backs
And ride for several furlongs out of town
Along the muddy roads and mountain tracks,
Wearing a grim and terrifying frown.
Months later all the females have attacks
And call the coypu doctors to their beds.
What's born has dreadful capybara heads.

James Fenton, 'The Wild Ones'

For as long as I can remember I have had an abiding love of motorcycles and the people who ride them. As a kid I'd hang around outside the local bike shop clutching my *I Spy Motorcycles* book, eagerly noting down details of the various makes and models, asking silly questions of their owners and breathing in the heady atmosphere of chrome, oil and noise. So I guess I can truthfully lay claim to have been researching the 'motorcycle subculture' for almost three decades. In my wallet I carry a dog-eared photograph of me, aged two and a half, astride my uncle's 650 cc BSA. My old man sat on the pillion seat, while I happily twisted the throttle and presumably imagined my juvenile self belting off down the road. Even now, thirty years on, I still get the same feeling of exhilaration simply sitting on a bike. It's a feeling that, despite all my rigorous pseudo-scientific research into the phenomenon, I just can't manage to dispel or even begin to understand. Hopefully, I never will.

I bought my first bike two weeks before my sixteenth birthday for the princely sum of £7. It was a 500 cc Ariel, old and much neglected but nevertheless, in my eyes, without a shred of

7

doubt, *the* most beautiful thing I'd ever seen. A builder mate of my old man's brought it home on the back of his lorry, while at the same time bending my ear about the folly of wasting good money on 'one of them death traps'. We heaved it down off the tailboard and propped it up against the garden wall, as the stand had somehow been lost in transit. The petrol tank promptly dropped to the ground with a sickening clang, which put a large dent in the side, and deposited its contents all over the path. Things didn't get off to a particularly great start. But there was worse to come, and I had hardly crossed the threshold before the arguments began.

Bear in mind that the year in question was 1965, and 1965 was the height of the mods' and rockers' crusades on the beaches of the nation. (I never could for the life of me understand why it was that in newspaper reports the mods always got their name put first.) That being so, anybody under the age of twenty-one who expressed interest, however remotely, in the ownership of a motorcycle ('family men' with double adult combos excluded) was generally considered to be, if not exactly a delinquent psychopath, at the very least some sort of social misfit. My own parents, in common with other *Daily Mirror*-reading parents throughout the land, felt that motorcycles, apart from being dirty and dangerous, represented a short cut to the magistrate's court.

On reflection, I suppose they may well have been right. Riding bikes has got me into more than a few scrapes over the years. I've got wet, cold and both wet and cold on them. I've pushed them for miles, cursed and sworn at them, bruised my knuckles on them, been in constant debt because of them, fallen off them more times than I care to remember and been arrested on them. I have also derived unimaginable pleasure from riding them, made many close friends through their ownership and seen sights and experienced things that I would never have encountered if I had taken my father's advice, waited the extra year and bought a car instead.

Even today, most people I come into contact with regard me as something strange and threatening despite the fact that I've got a university degree under my belt and do 'research' for that august body, the Economic and Social Research Council. People just can't understand why it is that I ride a bike and live the way I do. I get turned away from pubs and find it hard to get rented accommodation. I get stopped and searched by the police with monotonous regularity. And I still have difficulty in convincing people that I'm not about to punch them up in the air or steal their money. My mate Shaun is fond of telling me that it's 'the price we pay for the life we lead' and that it must be borne with good grace. I'm not so sure. One thing I do know is that if I ever had to make a choice between changing the way that I go about things in order to gain social acceptance – thus living a lie, remaining 'an outsider' – and being true to myself, then there really wouldn't be any contest at all, Anyway, it's fun making life hard for yourself, ain't it?

This book sets out to present what I hope will be a readable account of the origins and evolution of the 'biker lifestyle'. It is a lifestyle which I have had the immense good fortune to have lived to the full for nearly twenty years. More rubbish has been written about it, and more myths perpetuated, than practically any other modern social phenomenon. However, the aim hasn't been to set the record straight; I have no excuse to make to the general public regarding either our real or our imaginary behaviour. This isn't a confession. So if you're expecting to find lurid accounts of people biting the heads off live chickens or indulging in unspeakable sexual activities, I'm afraid that you're going to be out of luck. I leave all that to the 'experts' from the Sunday newspapers who seem to know so much more about what goes on than those who are actually involved. Nor should it be taken as an objective, in-depth, socio-psychological profile of the outlaw biker. It is simply my own view of a subculture which, during the past forty years, has spread halfway across the world and about which, despite high street visibility and continual media exposure, very little is known and still less understood.

My account finishes around 1968, not just because that's as far as I got before writing it became a pain in the arse but because 1968 was the year when the biker subculture, in common with every other subcultural movement in Western society, underwent a whole host of quite radical and lasting changes. And the pictures haven't been stuck in merely to fill up space; they represent an integral and vital part of the book. It would be absolutely out of the question to tackle a subject like the biker lifestyle without making at least some attempt to try to reproduce the unique atmosphere of that lifestyle as it is actually *lived* by its adherents. After all, the very act of riding a bike is itself an exciting and potentially dangerous experience. Unlike the car driver, the biker constantly exposes himself to the hazards of the road. Out there on the highway, winding it on, he is truly the master of his own destiny, a free-willed individual engaged in a relentless quest for the spirit of life. There are no half-measures. Like his cultural predecessor, the American Indian, he may go down, but he'll most certainly go down fighting.

FROM BRANDO TO BARGER:
THE EVOLUTION OF A MODERN-DAY OUTLAW

The angel rides with hunch-backed children, poison oozing from his engine.
Wieldin' love as a lethal weapon, on his way to a hubcap heaven.
Baseball cards poked in his spokes, his boots in oil he's patiently soaked
The roadside attendant nervously jokes as the angel's tires stroke his precious pavement
The interstate's choked with nomadic hordes
In Volkswagen vans with full running boards dragging great anchors
Followin' dead-end signs into the sores
The angel rides by humpin' his hunk metal whore.
Madison Avenue's claim to fame in a trainer bra with eyes like rain
She rubs against the weather-beaten frame and asks the angel for his name
Off in the distance the marble dome
Reflects across the flatlands with a naked feel off into parts unknown.
The woman strokes his polished chrome and lies beside the angel's bones.

Bruce Springsteen, 'The Angel'

There is no denying it. The bandit is brave, both in action and as victim.
He dies defiantly and well, and unnumbered boys from slums and
suburbs, who possess nothing but the common but nevertheless
precious gift of strength and courage, can identify themselves with him.
In a society in which men live by subservience, as ancillaries to
machinery, the bandit lives and dies with a straight back.[1]

'Hell's Angels make punks, mods and skinheads look like a bunch of choirboys,' said one of the few Welsh policeman to have first-hand experience of the motorcycle-borne gangs whose wild exploits make headline news.

Wales already has several motorcycle gangs but these are dismissed by police as a 'load of yobs and kids pretending to be something they've read about' and to call them Hell's Angels would be a dubious compliment to which they are not entitled.

These groups, according to a [police] spokesman . . . pose no big problem [to law and order]. 'We know them, we know their parents', he said. 'Most of them work and change into their biking gear when they clock off. If they go looking for trouble, they find we are there to stop them.

'A real Hell's Angels chapter would require different tactics – they can be vicious.'[2]

The *Western Mail*, reporting on 'the lawless cult that came from the States' in the wake of a 1980 Cardiff rape trial involving several members of the then 'unofficial' Windsor chapter of the Hells Angels. During the course of the trial, in which three of the five defendants were convicted and imprisoned, the seriousness of the incident escalated from a straightforward crime, ably handled by the Cardiff police, into a wholesale threat to law and order throughout the entire Principality. The police and media loudly disassociated their own home-grown 'yobs and kids', whose actions and motives they could understand, from the alien invaders, whose behaviour was as inexplicable as it was irrational. It was as if they needed to remind the good folks of South Wales of the terrifying consequences of lawlessness and immorality. In so doing, they boosted their own image as guardians of the public peace, conjuring up an abnormal 'barbarian other' which threatened their existence. In fact, the Cardiff area has for many years boasted the highest crime rate in Wales and, indeed, one of the highest in the whole of the United Kingdom. Incidents of violence and sexual attacks, if not exactly commonplace, are hardly a rare enough occurrence to warrant the kind of blanket press coverage surrounding this particular crime. What, then, was the extraordinary ingredient which caused such hysteria? What kind of people were these 'folk devils' who could instil fear into the hearts of the police and press of a nation? What is the reality behind the myth of biker subculture? Who are the real outlaw bikers?

The first myth that needs to be dispelled is that the Hells Angels Motorcycle Club is somehow representative of the entire motorcycle subculture. Numerous films, novels, press and police reports and sociological studies all claim to portray the authentic face of the biker as the ragged, unwashed, 'don't-give-a-shit' Hells Angel. But the subculture is more widespread. It encompasses, both structurally and historically, many recognizably different strands within its ranks. True, the Angels, more than any other body, epitomize the extreme, hard-core end of the spectrum. But they are only one group among many. They are probably the most notorious but certainly not wholly representative either of the 'outlaw' bike club or of 'outlaw' bikers in general.

Unfortunately the term 'Hells Angel' is ubiquitously used to describe any leather-jacketed individual, from fourteen to forty, whom the powers that be consider to be potentially antisocial, whether on or off a motorcycle. But the official Hells Angels Motorcycle Club is much more exclusive and probably has fewer than 2,000 members worldwide. The club's influence, both within the subculture and outside it, has been wide, but its public image owes more to the lurid fantasies of Hollywood movie moguls than to its own endeavours. It was perhaps this media vision of the archetypical 'outlaw' biker lifestyle during the 1960s that turned them into the world's number-one bike club. It also led many individual unaligned motorcycle riders in a host of countries to emulate their celluloid heroes and to form outlaw clubs known by a variety of names ranging from the sublime to the sheer bloody ridiculous: Galloping Gooses, Desperadoes, Outlaws, Heaven's Sinners, Angels of Death, Flaming Creatures, Huns, Renegade Nomads, Sons of Satan, Broad Jumpers, Flying Reptiles, etc., etc.

Thus, with the willing help of journalists and scriptwriters, the name 'Hells Angels' became synonymous with the expansion of a particular form of motorcycle subculture quite unlike any other that had gone before but which had existed on the West Coast of America in an embryonic form since the late 1940s.

The outlaw bike culture was born at the end of the Second World War. It grew in the run-down quarters of Los Angeles, Oakland, San Francisco and the many grey urban sprawls dotted along the Pacific Coast. California's golden dream did not reach far into the ghetto. Life there had progressively worsened during the immediate post-war years. Thousands of rural workers, weary of decades of trying to scratch a living from unproductive land, flocked to the towns in search of a piece of America's massive industrial expansion. The already seething mass of human misery was swollen to unbearable proportions by this influx. They constituted a massive new workforce to be ruthlessly exploited in factories and sweatshops. They were shunned by the more experienced and better organized section of the urban labour force and forced to live in conditions far worse than those of their sharecropping Okie cousins. Families were split up and traditional ties of mutual support and dependence severed. In this melting pot of humanity, each man competed against his neighbour to earn a living and to better himself.

In the land where 'any man could become President', the ideology of the ghetto was: work hard, keep your mouth shut, and hope that prosperity is just around the corner. This first generation of poor-white slum dwellers was quite unlike its much more experienced and culturally better adapted black and Mexican counterparts. It had yet to realize that there was no room for the sober, decent, individualistic human being in the new cut-throat world. The parents were anxious to maintain a sense of decency and clung to the values of their rural forefathers. Not so their offspring who, brought up in the ghetto, quickly learned to adopt the methods of defence and resistance of their black contemporaries and to spurn the lifestyle and dreams of their elders. The traditional values of life in small-town West Virginia or Alabama were as alien to them as little green men from Mars. They wanted no part of it and resorted instead to alternative ways of getting by and getting on. They fully realized the hopelessness of the situation they were in and understood only too well the gulf between their parents' aspirations and material reality.

We live on the edge of the coloured section of the city [Oakland]. My father had a job in a warehouse and my mother took in ironing. I watched them work harder and harder while we grew poorer and poorer. If it hadn't been for my ability to sneak into an occasional movie I would have grown up believing everyone lived more or less the way we did. We lived in a two-room apartment that always stank of dirty laundry and was overrun with filthy roaches that only the landlord had trouble seeing . . .

There were some guys on my block who had come out West with their families about the same time I did. They came to California to avoid starving, only to discover that you can starve in more ways than one . . . My folks starved to death; but it wasn't because they didn't have enough to eat. My friends and I would have starved just the way our folks did if we had to go on living the way people seemed to expect us to live. You're supposed to grow up quietly and get a stinking, petty

job and spend the rest of your life drinking beer in front of a TV, learning how to go on working and consuming and voting for the right thief.[3]

It was the cagey, street-wise hustler, the black 'dream seller' who lived fast and well or Brando's cool waterfront gang leader who became their heroes and teachers, not the fiery Bible-thumping preacher or the Cadillac-borne Wall Street corporation man. Machismo and cunning were the names of the game, the roads to respect, not hard work and decency – the rules were already drawn up. If the game was to be won, it had to be played the right way.

The Haves ran the world, dictating moral codes and standards of living that any decent self-respecting citizen had to live up to in order to be something other than 'trash'. Then, while the Have-Nots worked their guts out to maintain that minimum standard, trying in their own pathetic, dumb way to live up to moral codes etc., the people who made those codes broke every rule in the book behind the privacy of their locked penthouses and middle-class doors. You couldn't expect them to give anything away. Why should they? And you couldn't blame the Have-Nots for being too ignorant to see through the game. You couldn't put them down because they were simple and innocent. No, that's just the way the world went round. You could either go along or drop out of the race.[4]

What emerged, as one form of 'solution' to the problems faced by these disaffected first-generation white immigrants, was the arrival on the American scene of what was probably the first national post-war 'delinquent' subculture: the world of the motorcycle outlaw. Here was a way of life distinct and different from both the black culture of the ghetto and the parents' working-class culture. It was a way of life which owed nothing to the straight world of Middle America, yet it transcended the tenements and warehouses of downtown Oakland.

While the ghettos were bubbling all over the United States, thousands of young GIs were returning home. Having fought for 'freedom', they found that the world had moved on since 1941. Those that had stayed at home had taken their share of the jobs and the girls. Momma's apple pie and square dancing had suddenly become more than a little tame for travellers who had ventured beyond the county seat to Europe or South-East Asia. In a world where rock 'n' roll still hadn't been discovered by Alan Freed, where Frank Sinatra and Patti Page were the most exciting thing in socially acceptable white music, where James Dean was some years away from being a rebel (with or without a cause) and where Errol Flynn hadn't yet relinquished to Marlon Brando his status as the 'Wild One' of the silver screen, the disaffected white youth of urban America relieved their boredom by turning once again, as had their fathers in the 1930s, to the relatively affordable motorcycle as a means of mobility and excitement.

THE OUTLAW ROLLS INTO TOWN AND LIFE
WILL NEVER BE THE SAME AGAIN

He wore black denim trousers and motorcycle boots
And a black leather jacket with an eagle on the back
He had a hopped-up 'sickle that took off like a gun
That fool was the terror of Highway 101.
    The Cheers, 'Black Denim Trousers and Motorcycle Boots'

Motorcycle riders got together and formed clubs, hung out in bars, went away for weekends and occasionally raised a little hell. As time went on, a distinctive biker lifestyle began to emerge. Riders affected a similar style of dress and pattern of speech, and the clubs became more tight-knit and divorced from the world of the ride-to-work 'citizen' motorcyclist. Highly structured and highly visible clubs like the Booze Fighters, Galloping Gooses, 13 Rebels, Market Street Commandos, Satan's Daughters, Satan's Sinners, Winos and the Pissed-Off Bastards of Bloomington (later in 1948 to become the Berdoo founder chapter of the Hells Angels), began to travel a little further afield in search of excitement.

The appearance of a bunch of strange-looking city boys on noisy motorcycles was infinitely disturbing to small-town farming folk. For generations they had existed in a kind of time warp; their way of life, values, beliefs and institutions remaining largely untouched by the effects of the industrial revolution and two world wars. Few of them had even visited the urban sprawls of the Western seaboard, let alone made the acquaintance of city dwellers. They instinctively distrusted city ways of doing things. And yet suddenly here were some of the scroungiest-looking individuals they'd ever clapped eyes on right there in their own main street, laughing and drinking and hollering at each other in a language which bore little resemblance to the English taught in the town school. 'Better keep the children away from these goddam freaks – no telling what they

might do ... And where did they get the money for those big shiny motorsickles? Probably the proceeds of drug peddling, extortion, white slavery or something even worse. Better lock up your daughters, your wives, your property. You couldn't be sure just what these people were capable of ...' The fact that many of the riders had only recently been released from the service of Uncle Sam, having given their all to defend the very way of life, the values and the institutions that the townspeople enjoyed, was neither here nor there. Freedom meant the right to keep yourself to yourself, not a licence to go around scaring God-fearing folk half to death. No, it was no good trying to talk sense into these boys. They must be denied hospitality or they would return in greater numbers to wreak even greater havoc in the streets. 'If you let them get away with it once ...'

It was not long before the media and the law-enforcement agencies recognized a potential source of 'trouble' and decided to rise to the challenge posed to their authority by these un-American 'cycle bums'. Their method was systematic harassment. The result was the ostracism of the 'outlaw' bikers from the mass of 'law-abiding' motorcyclists and the subsequent emergence of a new American 'folk hero' or 'folk devil' (depending on your point of view or, more particularly, your social situation).

What occurred on a hot summer's day, 4 July 1947, was an event guaranteed to bring this new kind of motorized outlaw to the attention of the great American public. It was to provoke in moms and dads throughout the land a morbid dread of anyone sporting a leather jacket or driving anything with fewer than four wheels.

The concept of the 'motorcycle outlaw' was as uniquely American as jazz. Nothing like them had ever existed. In some ways they appeared to be a kind of half-breed anachronism, a human hangover from the era of the Wild West. Yet in other ways they were as new as television. There was absolutely no precedent, in the years after the Second World War, for large groups of hoodlums on motorcycles, revelling in violence, worshipping mobility and thinking nothing of riding five hundred miles on a weekend . . . to whoop it up with other groups of cyclists in some country hamlet entirely unprepared to handle even a dozen peaceful tourists. Many picturesque, outback villages got their first taste of tourism not from families driving Fords or Chevrolets, but from clusters of boozing 'city boys' on motorcycles.[5]

The bikers had made it to the big time. They had been 'discovered' in the town of Hollister, California, and branded by the national press as the biggest threat to the American way of life since the Japanese took it into their heads to bomb Pearl Harbor. In the next ten years the image they created of wild men on motorcycles was to become the subject of numerous books, films, television programmes, newspaper and magazine articles. It was an image which prompted lawmen and elected officials everywhere to take the view that if they didn't want their own town overrun by these degenerate hoodlums, they had better clamp down good and hard on any kid who even looked like he might ride a motorcycle.

Thus the image was guaranteed to receive a wider and wider audience. It was eagerly adopted by rebellious white ghetto kids who had nothing to do, nowhere to go and no future. It became the new American outlaw culture, taking over where Billy the Kid, Wild Bill Hickock and Jesse James had left off. The motorcycle became a symbolic release from the drudgery and dead-endedness of everyday life,

and a way of recreating a group identity which had come to be abandoned during their city-bound migration. An Oakland teenager, later to become a Hells Angels member, describes his reaction to the Hollister 'riot':

Anything that drove the officials wild made me feel good. The establishment had never done anything for me, and in my youthful anger and taste for rebellion, I saw them as responsible for the hardship and misery of my parents and others like them . . .
I [had] . . . the clipping from the San Francisco Chronicle *pertaining to the Hollister riot.*
'San Benito street was littered with thousands of beer bottles and other debris. There was no available estimate of the damage. At the height of the pandemonium the motorcyclists drove their vehicles into bars and restaurants, tossed beer bottles out of upper-floor windows, raced through traffic signals and defied the seven-man police force.'
The more Rivera told me about his gang and motorcycle outlaws in general, the more I came to idolize their way of life. They were outlaws like Jesse James and Pretty Boy Floyd. They were wild and reckless and they made their own laws . . . It wasn't true that crime didn't pay. In fact, the way I saw it, a life of crime and social defiance was the only dignified way of life left open to the true individual. Rivera owned a big Harley, resplendent with custom tank, chrome galore, ape-hangers, the whole works. He was so cool all the chicks in the neighbourhood wanted him . . . And why not? He was a hero. A man on his own feet with a snarl on his face and nothing but contempt for the world at large. In short, a true outlaw.[6]

What happened at Hollister on that summer's day long ago was not in fact spontaneous rioting by a mob who went there bent on causing trouble. Nor did the events that take place achieve anything like the magnitude with which subsequent reports, both official and unoffical, credited them. That is not to say that the good people of that sleepy Californian town had nothing to complain about: many were quite justifiably put out by the behaviour of some of the motorcyclists. But, equally, many who read the accounts in their morning papers failed to recognize it as being their own hamlet laid siege to by hundreds of lawless hellraisers. Nevertheless, the American media were anxious to lend weight to the public's fear of the new youth menace and to reassure citizens about the continued validity and sanctity of the 'American way of life'. They felt compelled to regale their readership with descriptions of the weekend's events that were, if not exactly fictitious, at the very least highly coloured and selective.

Life magazine of 21 July 1947 picked up on the furore and made sure that everybody from New Mexico to New York became aware of the potential threat to law and order precipitated by the Hollister events. Under a carefully posed photograph of a large gentleman on a motorcycle, clutching a bottle of beer in either hand, looking more like an off-duty truck driver than a 'wild-eyed barbarian', and replete with the requisite 'ordinary member of the public' looking on, it commenced its 'informed' article with the following words:

On the fourth of July weekend, 4,000 members of a motorcycle club roared into Hollister, California, for a three-day convention. They quickly tired of ordinary motorcycle thrills and turned to more exciting stunts. Racing their bikes down the main street and through traffic lights, they rammed into restaurants and bars, breaking furniture and mirrors. Some rested awhile by the curb (see photo). Others hardly paused. Police arrested many for drunkenness and indecent exposure but could not restore order. Frankly, after two days, the cyclists left with a brazen explanation, 'We like to show off. It's just a lot of fun.' But Hollister's police chief took a different view. Wailed he, 'It's just one hell of a mess.'[7]

Notwithstanding the fact that such a description didn't quite jell with the views of the events held by any of the participants involved in the affair – motorcyclists, police or public – the article predictably generated the response which *Life* was seeking. Not only were the 'rebels' castigated by 'ordinary decent people', together with their elected representatives and law-enforcement agencies, but also 'respectable' motorcycling organizations, notably the long-established American Motorcycle Association (AMA) who had convened the Hollister races, anxiously fell over itself in an attempt to dissociate both its organization and AMA members from the trouble-making 'outlaws' who had turned up uninvited. Letters in the following issues of *Life* summed up the feelings of its readers towards the perpetrators of those terrible deeds. Many correspondents pointed out that it was only a 'small minority' of non-AMA-affiliated motorcycle clubs which turned the event into the débâcle it became. The following letter is typical of the response:

There is a natural tendency [writes a Mr Wynn] when you first begin to ride a motorcycle to feel that you are above the crowd and consequently you may do many childish stunts to impress the bystander. However, the longer you ride, the healthier a respect you gain for the motorcycle itself and realize that you need possession of all your faculties to master this man-killer. Drinking beer, as our friend in the picture seems to be doing, is one of the fundamental 'don'ts' of riding.
I would like to mention some ... safe and sane Hollywood motorcyclists: Clark Gable, Larry Parks, Randolph Scott, Ward Bond, Andy Devine, Bob Stack; I could go on ad infinitum.[8]

And another letter, from a member of the 'motorcycling establishment', displayed particular hysteria:

Words are difficult [writes Paul Brokaw, editor

of Motorcyclist *magazine] to express my shock . . . We regret to acknowledge that there was a disorder in Hollister – not the act of 4,000 motorcyclists, but rather a small percentage of that number, aided by a much larger group of non-motorcycling hellraisers and mercenary-minded bar-keepers. We in no manner defend the culprits – in fact drastic action is under way to avoid recurrences of such antics. You have, however, in presentation of this obnoxious picture, seared a pitiful brand on the character of tens of thousands of innocent, clean-cut, respectable, law-abiding young men and women who are the true representatives of an admirable sport.*[9]

Life's 'authoritative' account of the damage and chaos which resulted in 'nearly a hundred jailed cyclists and almost as many injured' was widely publicized. But as Hunter Thompson points out:

A hastily assembled force of only twenty-nine cops had the ['riot'] . . . under control by noon of July 5th. (And by nightfall that day, the main body of motorcyclists had left town.) Those who stayed behind did so at the request of police; their punishment ranged from $25 traffic fines to ninety days in jail for indecent exposure (the natural result of the imbibing by the motorcyclists of excessive quantities of beer, supplied to them by 'disgusted' traders). Of the 6,000 to 8,000 people supposedly involved in the fracas, a total of 50 were treated for (minor) injuries at the local hospital.[10]

Surprise, surprise, no convictions for serious or violent crimes. Unless you happen to include indecent exposure in such a context as a particularly offensive act, you must surely be forced to conclude either that *Life's* correspondent was deaf, blind, daft or drunk himself or that the magazine had deliberately sought, for reasons of its own, to create some sort of moral panic in the mind of its readership.

Nevertheless, no matter in whose interests *Life* had acted in publishing its report, the 'out-

siders' had been labelled well and truly as deviants, and that label was to stick fast. The word had been spread and fell on receptive ears. All over America 'concerned citizens' met to voice their opinions on the motorcycle thugs and prepared for assaults on their own towns. Town councils drafted legislation aimed specifically against bikers. Sheriffs, deputies, state police and National Guardsmen tensed their muscles to repel the invaders. Meanwhile, all over America, working-class boys dreamed of buying motorcycles, emulating the 'heroes' of Hollister and having a concerted dig at small-town values and morality. The message was both received and understood.

Sure enough, some two months later, Riverside, California, the host town of another AMA gathering, bore witness to a sequence of events similar to those of Hollister. This time two people lost their lives in drunken motorcycle accidents. In following summers Ensenada in New Mexico, Riverside again and Porteville, California, played unwilling hosts to motorcyclists who proudly claimed to be 'veterans' of the Hollister débâcle. The fight was on, and the national press was making a meal of it. Lines of battle were being drawn up with the active assistance of both the police and the AMA.

The statement of Sheriff Carl F. Bayburn of the Riverside Police Department received nationwide publicity:

He denounced the [offending] cyclists as 'riff-raff and hoodlums'.
He made it clear, however, that the majority of the cyclists were not of this type. 'They took the sport seriously,' he said, 'and had parked their equipment and registered at local hotels for a good night's sleep. The rioters,' he went on, 'do not belong to any recognized motorcycle group.'[11]

Sheriff Bayburn was supported in his views by Riverside Police Chief J. A. Bennet who, for the first time, publicly attributed the disruption caused to 'outlaw' clubs, a description which those involved were more than happy to have foisted upon them. He laid the blame for the 'rioting and trouble that turned the city's downtown section into a madhouse for three straight days' at the feet of 'a small minority of the visiting motorcyclists', but pointed out that the event's sponsor, the American Motorcycle Association, was composed of 'law-abiding sportsmen'.

He said that of the estimated 3,000 to 5,000 cyclists who attended, only a small number had misbehaved. 'A small percentage of members from "outlaw" clubs have insisted on endeavoring to ruin the show ... this group has dogged [the AMA's] tracks whenever they stage an event. Their purpose is to discredit the *bona fide* cycling association.'[12]

The AMA, for its part, went one step further. In response to politicians throughout the golden state who saw in the series of biker 'riots' an opportunity to jump on the bandwagon and push the 'law-and-order' crusade, the motorcycling organization responded to the call for the banning of its events by attempting to isolate the 'hooligan element' even further. When the League of California Cities called for a statewide ban on motorcycle race meetings, the AMA issued a much publicized press statement declaring its intention to outlaw those clubs and individuals who were 'ruining the sport'. Its Executive Secretary, Linton A. Kuchler, told the press that his organization felt that 'the disreputable cyclists were possibly 1 per cent of the total number of motorcyclists at the time. Only 1 per cent of motorcyclists are hoodlums and troublemakers.'[13]

As Thompson rightly remarks, using the AMA's 1 per cent criterion, and taking the 1967 national figure for two-wheel registrations which stood at over 6 million, 60,000 outlaws would have taken to the highways in that year alone – hardly an insignificant figure. The actual numbers involved in the incidents were not very important. What was of greater and lasting significance was that in its attempt to exonerate itself from any responsibility for the 'hoodlums and troublemakers', the AMA unwittingly created a collective badge of identity for its less than respectable hangers-on. It was hoist by its own petard. Far from feeling suitably chastened by the AMA's condemnation, the dissident motorcyclists were proud to accept their alienation and promptly adopted the '1 per center' symbol as a mark of their separation from the straight bikers they so much despised. Having been thus publicly labelled, the 'deviant' minority first took to wearing the '1 per center' patches on their jackets and then self-consciously set about forming themselves into a tremendous proliferation of clubs. These new clubs would not have to rely upon the AMA to provide venues where they could get together and do their own thing – pursuing the kinds of activities which the media, the police and the AMA had largely defined as appropriate behaviour for 'outlaw' bikers.

George Wethern, later to become Vice-President of the Oakland Chapter of the Hells Angels, recalls the outlaws immediate reaction to police harassment and, in particular, to the AMA statement:

A conference was held in San Francisco between the Hells Angels' statewide leadership including representatives from southern California ... [and the] leaders of clubs like the Gypsy Jokers, Road Rats, Galloping Gooses, Satan's Slaves, a North Beach club called the Presidents and Mofos, a funky outfit that looked more like winos than bikers ...

It was a historic gathering, sort of like the Yalta conference. Clubs that had traded stompings and chain whippings for years were parleying over a mutual problem ... 'We gotta stop fighting ourselves and start fighting these cops,' we'd say as the [wine] jug was passed. Everyone related instances of over-zealous law enforcement and downright frame-ups. And we kicked around a hostile statement from the American Motorcycle Association, the Elks Club of biking, which drew a distinction between its members and us renegades, and which characterized 99 per cent of the country's motorcyclists as clean-

*living folks enjoying pure sport. But it
condemned the other 1 per cent as antisocial
barbarians who'd still be scum riding horses or
surfboards.*

*The Angels and our friends, rather than
being insulted, decided to exploit the growing
tribute. We voted to ally under a '1 per center'
patch. As a supplement to regular colours, it
would identify the wearer as a righteous
outlaw. The patch also could help avoid
counterproductive in-fighting because an
Angel, Mofo or any 1 per center would be
banded against a common enemy.*

*Everyone knew the patch was a deliberately
provocative gesture, but we wanted to draw
deep lines between ourselves and the
pretenders and weekenders who only played
with motorcycles . . .*

*We were beginning to believe in our own
mystique. As we stacked a few rules and
rituals on the simple foundation of motorcycle
riding, we thought we were building a little
army.*[14]

It was left to Hollywood to put the icing on the
cake and to create, once and for all, the defini-
tive image of this new breed of motorcyclists –
the lawless rebels of the highway who, respect-
ing no one but their own kind, hunted in packs,
preying on all who had the effrontery to stand
up for decency, morality and property rights –
in short, 'the Wild Ones'.

BRANDO VINTAGE 1953: THE MENACE
IN YOUR OWN MOVIE THEATRE

Four of us downshifting/four/three/two/one
exhausts backing off/rumbling/rolling/throttles
the line of faces outside the neighbourhood theatre
turning towards our machines/us/the menace
feet down/rolling back wheels to the curb
hit kill buttons/pull compression releases
in unison/parked all in a neat row
shucked off gloves/stomped to the window in boots
    with popcorn there was a stupid love story
then they came/down the road/Brando riding
a Triumph/trophy taped to the bars/serious
riding the wrong lane/defying traffic
riding a pretty square bike/all road equipment
a serious look on his puffy boyish face
but riding the way we'd always wanted to
not giving a damn/we knew/we knew
    and those other freaks/Marvin's riding circus
clowns/what was their game?/their future?
stripped bikes/dragging for beers/riding
right into the tavern/who were they?
    later/swaggering out/kicking it like Brando
riding cool/turning it on down dark streets
we knew they'd finally made a real bike film
we knew we'd seen something. . . .
          Albert Drake, 'On Seeing *The Wild One*'

Brando was cast in the role of Johnny, leader of the Black Rebels Motorcycle Club. Resplendent in black leather jacket, denim jeans, and boots, topped off with a peaked cap pulled down low, he epitomized, in the eyes of the great American public, the real motorcycle-borne outlaw. (The British Board of Film Censors, in their infinite wisdom, felt the movie 'undesirable for general exhibition' until some fifteen years after its release in the United States). Like *Easy Rider*, a generation later, *The Wild One* created the image of the motorcyclist that haunted the minds and the writings of script-writers for years to come. Brando did for biking what Presley had done for rock 'n' roll, and

there was no turning back. What did it matter if the image didn't exactly tally with reality? Who cared whether the ragged, swaggering, drunk Chino, played by Lee Marvin, leader of a rival bike gang, portrayed a far more accurate picture of the kind of individual responsible for the 'invasions' of Hollister, Porteville or Riverside? It was Brando, the mean, moody, magnificent rebel who became the stereotype upon which the universalized mass motorcycle subculture of the late 1950s and 1960s was founded.

From its origins in Northern California the idea of a subcultural style, available to all who chose to adopt it, was catapulted on to the national, and then the international, scene. The more extreme precursors of the motorcycle subculture still survived, however, as the bogeymen of Middle America, the 'stars' of many a dubious work of fiction and second-rate 'B' movie, eventually to form the nucleus of the biker revival of the late 1960s. But meanwhile the media image stood unchallenged – Dylan's classic combination of 'the black-madonna motorcycle two-wheeled gypsy queen/and the silver-studded phantom who causes the grey-flannel dwarf to scream'[15] evoked the image that 'fitted', not only among the clientele of the hamburger joints of downtown Chicago, New York or Detroit but also in the coffee bars and juke-box dives bordering London's North Circular Road. At the Ace café and the Busy Bee, 'ton-up boys' practised their scowls in Seven-Up mirrors before donning their converted milkman's caps and blasting off into the night along rain-washed tarmac to invade Bethnal Green, Romford or who knows where.

The day had dawned when the motorcycle ceased, for all time, to be exclusively either cheap ride-to-work transport for the financially hard-pressed manual worker or the sporting mount of the more adventurous bourgeois. It became instead the object by which a specifically working-class subcultural style was generated and sustained. It was a commodity reappropriated and redefined until it came to represent a symbol of resistance to the all-embracing hegemony of the dominant culture. The motorbike, which was both relatively cheap and readily available, became not only a source of previously denied mobility but also, much more importantly, the nuts and bolts around which the everyday leisure activities of a significant sector of working-class youth came to be organized.

The arrival of the motorcycle as a means of transport materially accessible to the mass of working-class youth – in America during the mid-1940s and a decade later in Europe – meant, for the first time, that the horizons of leisure activity were extended beyond the confines of the local high-street café or dance hall. Over and above this new-found freedom of mo-

bility, the motorcycle offered a 'magical release' from the prison of work-a-day life. To ride a motorcycle meant much more than driving the family saloon – it was exciting, it was noisy, it was brash and, what's more, it got up the nose of authority. To ride a motorcycle, and to ride it in a fashion that displayed an obvious contempt for both personal safety and the exigencies of the Highway Code, was in itself rebellious. The more Joe Public was shocked and irritated by the spectacle, the better it felt. So what if you were only a warehouse boy who spent fifty hours a week, every week, sweeping floors and loading lorries? So what if you got shouted at all day by the foreman and all weekend by your old man? At night, gunning it on under the neon lights of the freeway, the wind tugging at your hair and your girl close-pressed behind you, you were a king – and nobody or nothing could take that away. You didn't have to take your problem to the United Nations; you could banish the 'Summertime Blues' just by twisting back the throttle and watching the speedo needle arc its way across the dial towards oblivion. To hell with the danger. So long as Buddy, Richie and the Big Bopper were up there watching over you – like rock 'n' roll, you'd never die – nothing could go wrong. And if it did? Heaven had to be better than Berdoo or, for that matter, Battersea. And the Teen Angel was ready at the gates waiting, golden-haired, open-limbed and open-hearted, for all those who dared defy mortality. The motorcycle was your own reality, and the motorcycle subculture offered a status which transcended that ascribed to you by your social position. Your mates knew how you felt, even if nobody else in the world cared a damn, and to be something in their eyes became the only thing that mattered.

There's no experience [writes one teenage convert] like riding a [bike]. It's a huge, sleek and sinister brute, capable of amazing feats of power and speed. As soon as I felt comfortable and began to adjust to the machine, I found myself cranking it on, letting off and cranking on again ... I was stepping over the threshold, passing from my earthbound, slovenly existence into a world of strength, speed and prestige. The [bike] as a status symbol, indeed. Wherever I went, coasting along, people turned their heads to stare. Some of them openly envious, others interested, and some obviously appalled, but there was a common reaction in all of them. They either envied me or were afraid of me. Before I had the bike I was a nothing. A nameless face in the crowd. A ragged urchin from the streets who didn't belong anywhere and would never amount to anything. The [bike] changed all that. Now I was something ... somebody.[16]

It is not, of course, contended that this entire subcultural explosion can be traced solely to the release of *The Wild One*. However, the film projected the image which brought together many separate strands of development in the motorcycle subculture. It was an image which fitted a particular conjectural moment and which stuck mainly because of the immediate and overwhelming reaction that Brando's outlaw received from a hysterical media.

The film itself, if viewed today, appears innocuous enough. The fight scenes have an obviously stage-managed character and there is a noticeable absence of either bad language or gratuitous violence. Indeed, when in 1968 the British Board of Film Censors finally relented and granted the film an 'X' Certificate, and it duly arrived at the Columbia, Shaftesbury Avenue, the reception given to it by Fleet Street was very tame indeed. The unanimous verdict was summed up well by the *Daily Express* headline 'THE WILD ONE IS SUCH A MILD ONE.' But although in retrospect it might seem rather a quaint, if interesting, period piece, in the highly charged atmosphere of public condemnation following the wave of biker riots in the late 1940s and early 1950s, it went down with American cinema-goers like the Chinese invasion of Korea. It was based loosely on a little-known and best forgotten Hollister-in-

spired story called 'Cyclist Raid', written by Frank Rooney and published in the January 1951 issue of *Harper's* magazine. In the words of producer Stanley Kramer, it 'touched [his] sense of social responsibility'.[17]

The Wild One tells the by now familiar story of two groups of bikers who take over a sleepy Midwestern town and proceed to race around at breakneck speed demolishing everything in sight and subjecting the patient townspeople to torrents of (very seemly) abuse. After much marauding and brawling the sheriff's daughter, her father no longer able to cope, manages to persuade the villain of the error of his ways. Johnny (Brando) promptly falls in love with her, renounces his past life and turns against Chino (Marvin), his incorrigible arch-rival. Then, in true 'folk devil' fashion, far beyond the appeal of reason, he drives the usurper out of town, thereby earning the eternal gratitude of the decent folks and proving to one and all that good inevitably triumphs over evil.

Unfortunately, this sterling message was lost on the great American public, and the only thing that managed to get through was the alarming vision of lawless gangs of leather-clad, amoral, inarticulate yobbos who could, with little opposition, run amok in civilized American towns. The same message was received and understood not only by redneck, patriotic John Birchers but also by those who relished the prospect of shocking their moral and political guardians by indulging in similar behaviour. As *Life* magazine, in its twenty-fifth anniversary issue of July 1972, put it: '*The Wild One* became a milestone in movie history, launching the cult of gang violence in films. It also helped create an image of motorcycling that non-violent bike riders have been trying to live down for a quarter of a century now.'[18]

Kramer, however, stoutly maintained that the film, as originally conceived, 'understood and captured a tear in the fabric of society' and hence represented an attempt to heal the split between young and old before it was too late. He says, 'There was no glorification of violence ... we simply showed that this was the first indication that a whole set of people were going to divorce themselves from society and set up their own standards.' So, where did he go wrong? How did the message become so incredibly distorted?

The Wild One encountered mammoth problems in the making. Kramer recalls:

I gathered together a band of motorcyclists – a gang just like the one that made the newspapers earlier . . . Brando and I talked to them, and then the writer Ben Maddow was brought in. But he was subpoenaed by the House of Un-American Activities Committee · . . . So John Paxton took over the script.

These guys were a new breed, and there weren't many of them around . . . They all had girls and were living like nomads. A lot of the dialogue is taken from our actual conversation with them. All the talk about 'We gotta go, that's all . . .' 'Just gotta move on' was something we heard over and over. And one· of the most famous lines in the film came from my conversation with them, too. I asked one of the kids, 'What are you rebelling against?' and he answered, 'What have you got?'

Well, we ran into trouble with the censors, who said that it was an anti-American, Communist film! In the original version, we told the truth about the incident – that no charges were brought against the boys because they brought so much business to the town! But the censors said this was unsuitable! They made us cut it out . . . [19]

Kramer's social message was, in the suffocatingly narrow world of film-making in the 1950s, both unacceptable and unfashionable, and his honesty was condemned as 'un-American'. It most certainly wasn't the message that the authorities wanted to hear, true or otherwise. Sadly, but inevitably, bigotry ruled the day. His hands were well and truly tied. He could either portray his teenage rebels the way that the censors wanted or pack the film in completely. His decision to capitulate to the opposition and re-think the whole project is echoed by the words of Johnny in the opening moments of the film: 'Once the trouble was under way, I just went along with it.'

By 'just going along with it' himself, Kramer was to create a monster which would take years to put down.

Thus, via a process of action and reaction, the motorcycle subculture evolved, in less than a decade, from a few relatively small groups of ex-GI bike riders into a mass subculture spreading far beyond the confines of California across the whole of North America and into Europe and Australasia. As the young bike-riding population expanded, a previously ailing motorcycle industry rubbed its hands with scarcely concealed delight and rapidly geared itself up to produce the kinds of machine and to project the kind of image that they felt would appeal to this newly created leisure market.

In America the two giants which had dominated the home market for nearly half a century, Harley-Davidson and Indian, were hard hit as their major British competitors – Triumph, BSA, Norton, Ariel, Matchless, AJS, Royal Enfield – realizing the vast sales potential of their products, exported cosmetically redesigned models in their thousands. Gimmicky advertising campaigns were employed to convince the American consumer that anyone who swung a leg over a motorcycle could become an instant rebel without being remotely antisocial. With the aid of clever copywriting, the motorcycle was fast transformed into the new 'fun machine', capable of making the most dedicated corporation man feel young and virile even if he was fat, pushing forty and well on the way to his first coronary. 'GO FARTHER FASTER ON A TRIUMPH AND GET THERE IN STYLE', 'MATCHLESS SORTS OUT THE MEN FROM THE BOYS', screamed the messages on the hoardings. The industry threw its weight behind the campaign to make the motorcycle rider once more a respectable member of society and, in so doing, further isolated those individuals who, through their behaviour, had placed themselves beyond the pale of civilized society.

The Europeans ... were not about to let pass the opportunity to stuff the coffers with American dollars provided by power-hungry colonials ...

The changes came, [they] smoothed out their engines, padded the seats of their fire-belchers, and tried, though they often failed, to cure their oil leaks.

The machines from England became a status symbol among riders ... And all three major British companies resorted to the American style of advertising.

Loud claims of power vied for attention. Colour photography displays abounded. There were contests and freebies given to bike buyers. Warranties were advertised. Accessories included, after-sale service promised, regular tune-ups offered. Free gas. Free helmets. Free jacket patches, passes for races, dates, driving lessons, insurance advice ... [20]

However, despite the progressive re-assimilation by the dominant culture of the motorcycle as an approved commodity, the problem of the recalcitrant minority of motorcycle-borne troublemakers was not so easily overcome. *The Wild One* was far from having been laid to rest, as the onset of the 1960s would show. Outlaw clubs continued to spring up, composed of riders who were proud to be different, imitating not Brando – the image that had been twisted, distorted and made decent for public consumption – but Marvin, the rebel who refused to conform. For the moment the beast had been held in check, but only for the moment. And meanwhile, across the Atlantic, it was only just beginning to bare its teeth ...

8

10

12

15

18

16

19

17

20

23

24

14 JOHN & HIS 117MPH CSR

28

29

30

32

38

40

42

44

46

47

50

53

52

58

59

65

66

68

HARLEY'S
BEST
FUCK
THE REST

HARLEY-DAVIDSON
CYCLES

WARNING!
IF YOU VALUE YOUR LIFE
AS MUCH AS I VALUE
THIS BIKE
DON'T FUCK WITH IT!

69

MOTORCYCLES..
A WAY OF LIFE

71

HARLEY FUCKING DAVIDSON

72

My best
Friend

N T

BIKERS BY
APPOINTMENT
ONLY

74

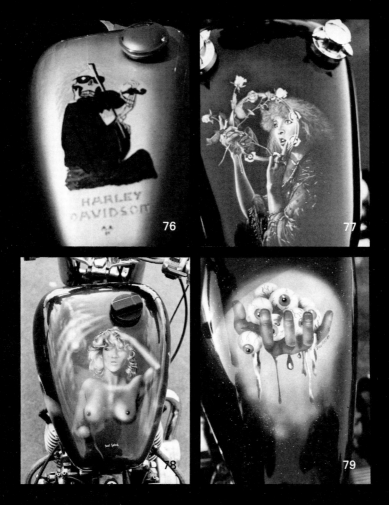

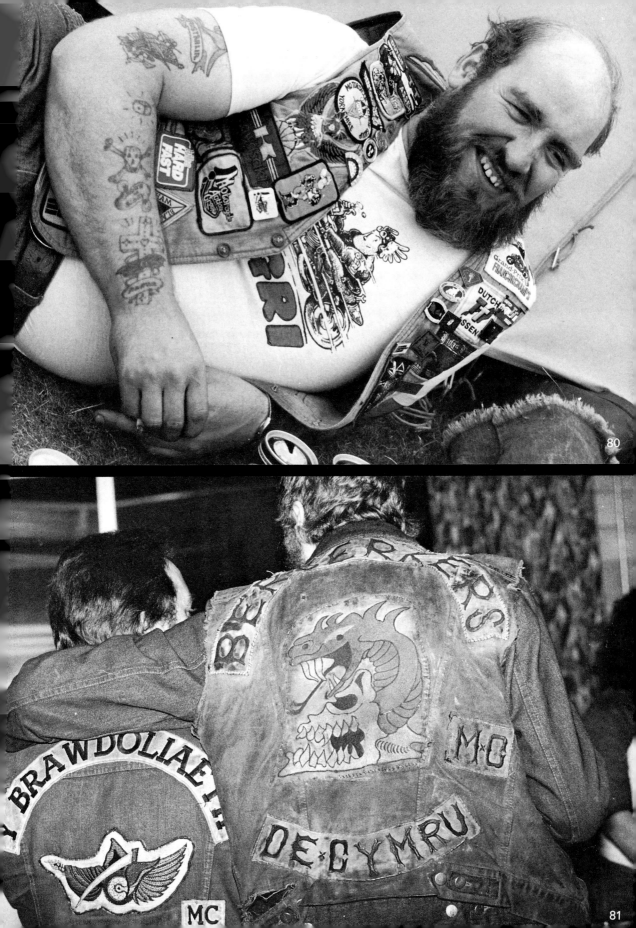

83

84

SUPPORT YOUR LOCAL HELLS ANGELS

87

HONDA'S MADE TO KEEP ASSHOLE'S OFF OF HARLEY-DAVIDSONS

89

MY DAD IS A HELLS ANGEL

88

DUDLEY PERKINS CO. 66 PAGE ST. SAN FRANCISCO

90

92

93

96

98

99

100

101

102

104

109

110

111

115

THEY'VE CLOSED
SORBONNE MADRI
BERLIN LAW FACU
HORNSEY COLUMB
MEXICO TOKYO
GUILDFORD AND M
LSE - SOLIDARIT
WITH LSE ST

117

116

118

119

BANDS & MAJORETTE

Norton

120

123

125

124

126

134

HELMETS CAN KILL
COMPULSION IS MANSLAUGHTER

CLEVELAND M.A.G RIDE FREE

CLEVELAND M.A.G.

130

135

133

132

138

HA HA HA HA HA, WIPE-OUT: THE COFFEE-BAR COWBOY BECOMES THE LEADER OF THE PACK

The dance was ending as they burst into the hall. They stood silently, staring, not moving yet somehow on the point of motion, like preying animals, fifteen or twenty boys wearing motorcycle kit. Their hair was greased and combed into styles called College Cut and Latin Cut and Campus Cut and Perry Como. Their expression was contemptuous and excited. A record of 'Good Night, Sweetheart', sung by Vera Lynn, was being amplified by the loudspeaker equipment attached to the wall above the door.

Someone shouted derisively, 'Call that dancing?'

'My mum could do better.'

'Come on Dad, move your fat arse.'

One of them, . . . suddenly seemed to become the leader . . . His jacket had a tiger's head painted on the back, his black leather jeans were stuffed into ex-army dispatch-rider's boots. He moved swiftly to the radiogram and, swinging his leg back, brought his boot crashing into the fan-shaped grill, splintering the wood and tearing the beige canvas material behind it.

The other boys surged forward on to the floor. Six of them paired and started to jive. Another used the panelling of the door as a sounding board to beat out a rhythm.

'Come on', yelled the leader . . . 'Let's do it over.'

He picked up a folding wooden chair and brought it down on top of the gramophone. The vicar advanced with his palms outstretched as if to calm them down.

'Boys, boys. Please. Let's not have any of the rough stuff.' [21]

Corny dialogue, maybe, but this description, penned in 1961, of the wrecking of a church youth club by 'mindless leather-jacketed yobbos' captures very well the quintessential image conjured up by the ton-up boys of the later 1950s – an image which was guaranteed to shock and dismay a British public still unable to come to terms with the realization that the Suez crisis had finally sounded the death knell of a glorious colonial past.

In a Britain emerging from the upheaval of the Second World War, where traditional working-class patterns of life were in a state of flux, there evolved a series of delinquent subcultures which attempted to 'defend, symboli- cally, a constantly threatened space and a de- clining status,'[22] by adopting distinctive styles and 'group-minded behaviour as a readily avail- able, albeit imaginary solution,' to the problems encountered in material life which remained in- soluble'.[23]

The austerity and drabness of those im- mediate post-war years cast a cheerless grey mantle over the whole of British society – ration books, clothing coupons, bomb sites, pre-fabs, make-do-and-mend, queue for this, queue for that, queue for every other bloody thing. People were glad to be alive, if you could call it living; glad to get back to normal. But what was nor- mal? Normal was just a memory, a faded photograph on the parlour wall. Normal was gone for ever, buried beneath a hail of German bombs, shot to pieces on the battlefields of Europe and North Africa. Normal was shattered, bent, twisted, distorted and mutilated beyond all recognition. Normal was dead. But the older generation stubbornly refused to believe the evidence before their eyes and carried on going through the motions. They knuckled down, unquestioning and uncomplaining, sustained by an unshakeable conviction that everything would turn out all right in the end. With a combination of Almighty God on the one hand and the Welfare State on the other, the old way of life would be rebuilt, brick by brick, if necessary. It was only a question of time.

But the young, born and raised in the turmoil of war, were not so sure. They had no roots, no golden past to recapture. The days of the British Empire were as remote to them as ancient Rome. Fifteen years or 1,500 years, the past was history, irrelevant. The only thing that mattered was now. Life was for living, not for reminiscing. The older generation had had their go, and look what a mess they'd made of the world. They'd fucked it up good and proper. Now it was up to the kids to have a go. There were jobs to be had and money to be earned. Maybe money could not buy happiness, but what it could buy certainly felt good. The older generation didn't understand, couldn't understand, wouldn't understand. As the song said:

Saturday night and I just got paid
Fool about my money, don't try to save.
My heart says go, go have a time.
It's Saturday night and, baby, I feel fine . . .[24]

Who the hell needed 'security'? Security meant being tied down, 'planning for the future'. Who cared about the future anyway? The future, like the past, could take care of itself.

The teds were the first group to be associated with a unique subcultural style, the appearance of which was to generate a considerable adverse societal reaction, similar to that which marked the emergence of its American contem-

porary, the biker subculture. Teds quickly became associated, in the minds of the public, with gang violence and a decline in moral standards. They were the archetypal 'bad boys' of the 1950s. Even the most minor incident involving youths whose dress could be held to resemble the ted style received widespread alarmist publicity in the media, and the status value of such newsworthiness was not lost on the teds themselves. As T.R. Fyvel notes in his book *The Insecure Offenders*, the wave of rock 'n' roll riots that took place in British cinemas in 1955 appears to have been precipitated largely by a hysterical over-reaction to uproarious behaviour at the Elephant and Castle's Trocadero Cinema during a showing of Bill Haley's film *Rock Around the Clock*. The series of cinema riots throughout the country which followed in its wake exhibited an almost carbon-copy similarity to the Elephant and Castle riot, just as if the media had defined and communicated the sort of behaviour that was appropriate for teds to indulge in. Fyvel quotes a local social worker who held the opinion that

that excitement and sense of destruction were fed by publicity. The gangs felt that such behaviour was almost expected of them.

. . . they began to behave more defiantly, to show off, to be 'big-heads', to become what they thought the public wanted them to be – cosh boys, Teddy boys. It was as if they were being sucked into violence by something bigger than themselves.

In other words, press publicity itself sharpened the lines of conflict between society and Teddy boys.[25]

The escalation of the teddy-boy 'problem' was brought about through a process of action and reaction similar to that which marked the expansion and solidification of the biker subculture in the wake of the Hollister riot – the more the media played upon the stereotypical image of the ted, the more rebellious working-class youth became. But, inevitably, as greater and greater numbers of youths adapted to the style, clothing manufacturers and record companies, with an eye to exploiting this new market potential, began to produce teddy-boy fashion clothes and commercial rock 'n' roll in mass quantities. Thus the subculture gradually lost its cohesive force – its main impetus, the distinctive 'uniform' of the ted and its previously 'barbaric' music becoming, if not exactly culturally acceptable, at least tolerable. By the end of the decade the original rebellious image of the ted was diffuse and dated, and apart from a few dyed-in-the-wool rock-a-billies, the subculture had in effect ceased to exist.

The Teddy boys in their early large groups, at the height of the vogue, had a fierce sense of being an outcast community. They cultivated this sense, they depended on it, their revolt had its esprit de corps *and went with rigid loyalties of members towards each other. However, when large numbers of boys took up the fashion, so that it was no longer easy to tell who was 'a true Teddy boy' and who was not, the Teddy boys themselves were no longer a community 'which stood up against society in loneliness'. As the wearers of the garb became more numerous, the original gang spirit and cohesion was lost, and the large group broke up into smaller groups linked by definite aims.*[26]

One such group, centred on a particular form of activity which emerged out of the ted subculture and went on to replace it in the public mind as the new threat to civilized society, was the ton-up boys, the coffee-bar cowboys, the motorized maniacs who would belt you with a bike chain as soon as look at you . . .

While the teds restricted their nefarious activities to cinemas and dance halls, with the occasional racist attack thrown in for good measure, this new breed of 'juvenile delinquents' was quick to exploit rhe mobility offered by bikes, venturing beyond the working-class communities which spawned it to spread its message of nonconformity in pastures new. The middle classes had lost their geographical insulation, coming, for the first time, face to face with the 'folk devil'. Predictably they took exception to what they saw. That spectre, which had previously confronted them at arm's length in the morning paper or on the radio newsreel, now mocked them on the streets. It roared defiantly past the family car on Sunday afternoon outings or swaggered its way along the sea front at the popular resorts. It seemed to take childish delight in ridiculing the conventions of 'normal' people. It hunted in packs, made its presence as obtrusive as possible, played its music too loud, had little respect for law and order, and its morals were questionable, to say the very least.

Teds took to bikes naturally and easily. Bikes fitted the image – the driving beat of rock 'n' roll in motion – and black leather gear looked pretty neat into the bargain. Before long anyone young who rode a motorcycle and wore leather jacket and jeans (eminently practical motorcycling gear) posed a threat to the British way of life – a threat similar to the one Hitler had posed a decade or so previously. It was no longer safe to travel abroad on a Bank Holiday without being met with the disturbing sight and sound of wild young men and women who appeared 'too openly to flaunt the work and leisure ethic'. In the words of Stan Cohen, these people:

symbolized something far more important than what they actually did. They touched the delicate and ambivalent nerves through which post-war social change in Britain was experienced. No one wanted depression or austerity, but messages about 'never having it so good' were ambivalent in that some people were . . . [appearing to have] it too good and too quickly . . . Resentment and jealousy were easily directed at the young, if only because of their increased spending power and sexual freedom.[27]

This desperado-type image was fired by the imagination of the gentlemen of the press. In their eagerness to outbid each other with 'exclusive' revelations about the ton-up boys, they invented tales of ritualistic violence and death-defying stunts – for example the legendary but largely fictitious 'chicken run' in which two motorcyclists engaged in mortal combat by riding head-on towards each other, the rider who held his course the longer being declared the victor. In reality the behaviour of the motorcyclists of the period was, in the main, extremely mild indeed. The majority were more than happy simply to spend the evening down the 'caff', in the company of their mates, spinning yarns about the bikes they couldn't afford and the girls they'd never met except in their imagination.

Off down to the coast at weekends. Brighton, Margate, Southend, Blackpool, Yarmouth, Scarborough – it really didn't matter where, so long as you got away, shared a couple of beers with riders from elsewhere and had a good burn-up all the way there and back. The roar of a well-tuned engine was capable of transporting its owner to a plain of existence where the perennial problems of work, home and acne became meaningless. Being in motion was what it was all about. Tearing down the road at breakneck speed, or simply sitting in the steamy warmth of the caff, tapping your feet in time to the music, watching your mates flash past the window – it wasn't important how, where or why: you just had to keep moving. The races down to the roundabout and back before the record finished on the jukebox, the flat-out mass burn-ups along Murder Mile were branded as insanity by the 'outsiders' – those who always knew best what was good for you. But it wasn't insanity. It wasn't a search for death. It was a search for life, as much as anything. You were choosing your own way of life, maybe living it very dangerously, but that was your choice, and you would take your chances.

In England the pivotal skill was not brutality or dancing, but simply fast and dangerous riding ... every London hospital was crowded to overflowing with motorcycle casualties ... In the tangled mass of the road systems, the

jungle of glittering signs, the endless hypnotic cat's eyes, the monotonous lanes of traffic, the desolate ... cafeterias, the rockers were a strange and heartening breath of wildness and preserved integrity. They would come roaring down to London at the weekend in tribes, studs glittering, tangled greasy hair flying out behind them. There was something satisfying about the way in which a traffic stream on a hot Saturday, stalled, crammed with sweaty, pink families trapped with one another as the Mini-Minor was trapped in the queue, could be utterly negated, cancelled, by a clump of gleaming rockers hurtling past them to the roundabout.[28]

Life revolved around the caff. Pubs in those days (and these days) didn't welcome leather-jacketed bike riders with open arms. They upset the regular clientele, attracted the unwanted attention of the police and woke up the neighbours at stop-tap. The caff was where everything happened. It was warm and inviting and, best of all, it was cheap. With practice, you could avoid the watchful eye of the owner and make a cup of expresso coffee last an eternity. The time was spent chatting to mates or chatting up the birds who would hang around hoping to cadge a ride. The Ace, the Salt Box, Johnson's, the Nightingale, Chelsea Bridge tea stall, Quick Snacks, Box Hill – the names were legendary. Wherever you went there was always somebody you knew, somebody to talk bikes with. It was magic.

By the time the fifties gave way to the sixties, however, the impetus had slackened considerably. Cars were becoming more accessible to working-class youth. The once massive numbers who thronged the arterial-road coffee bars were fast undergoing a process of diffusion; new styles and forms of entertainment opened up alternative avenues of activity. The golden age of the bike caff was dead, killed off by a combination of diverse factors – pubs and clubs, wives and babies, jobs and cars, mortgages and mothers-in-law. Slowly but surely, the bike caffs were closing down. The image and the music were no longer considered cool; a jazzed-up Ford Consul was far better for pulling the birds than a clapped-out BSA and, in the days when respectable working-class parents frowned upon 'that sort of thing', offered much greater opportunities for sexual adventure. In 1963, Harry Johnson, the notoriously mean owner of Johnson's Café on the A20, just along the road from Brands Hatch, was ready to sell up. His nightly clientele had dwindled to a mere handful of two-wheeled enthusiasts, for whom the motorcycle represented more than a passport to instant status. Now, instead of the hundreds-strong Bank Holiday runs, it was more usual to see small bunches of riders in twos and threes making their way quietly and unceremoniously towards the coast, attracting little more than a passing glance from the general public.

Time rolled on, the kids got older and the, music changed. The familiar faces that had once thronged the caffs melted away. People made their excuses and simply dropped by the wayside – the spirit had gone. The collapse was inevitable. The bike scene had become cosy and complacent and was going absolutely nowhere. Nobody was sad about it – it just happened, that's all. What the hell, you can't go on living the same way for ever. Some of the boys got married to their steady birds, relegating their bikes to the shed at the bottom of the garden or saying goodbye to them completely as babies and mortgages came along in rapid succession. Others grudgingly surrendered to the years of subtly applied but abrasive pressure from parents or employers to mend their ways before it was too late. After all, you had to earn a living and get on in the world, hadn't you? It was all very well playing Jack the Lad, but it didn't get you anywhere in the long run, did it? *So why don't you come to your senses, boy? Those so-called mates of yours ain't gonna stick by you when you're in the shit, are they? Bunch of no-good layabouts, if you ask me. Never done a day's work since they were born. You're worth more than that, luv. Have your hair cut, get a nice suit, and we'll think about*

moving you up off the shop floor. Perhaps a trainee manager's position?

Not easy to hold out against such arguments when you're nineteen years old and potless. These were, after all, just ordinary working kids struggling to get along in the world. There was no real option: either they could do it the easy way by stepping back into line or they could do it the hard way and suffer for their sins. Middle-class youth could afford to be wayward. The sixties was their decade. Their subcultures were acceptable, fashionable, new and exciting. But for working-class youth those avenues of protest were effectively closed. Sooner or later they had to succumb to the inevitable steady job, wife and family. Some would slip through the net, but not many.

It was however, this hard core which was to reassert itself as the rockers of the early sixties. As Cohen states:

By 1964 [they] were dying out, but tough with the stubborn bitterness of a group left out of the mainstream of social change. Without the publicity that was given to the initial clashes with the Mods, their weakness would have become more apparent and they would have metamorphosed into another variant of the tougher tradition. Their very nature and origins made their chances of gaining strength autonomously [for example, by attracting new recruits] virtually out of the question.[29]

Strangely enough, it was the arrival on the scene of this new form of motorized subculture, the mods, which put biking in Britain back on its feet with a vengeance. Because without the appearance of the mods, the rockers would never have existed. And if the rockers had never existed...

It was the massive over-reaction of the media and the police, admirably documented in Cohen's *Folk Devils and Moral Panics*, to what was, in reality, little more than a series of relatively minor seaside skirmishes that revitalized the ailing motorcycle subculture and rallied thousands of new teenage recruits to the cause. To have the mods as an opposing force created a new sense of purpose, a new camaraderie and new possibilities for excitement. As Buttons, later to become President of the London founding chapter of the Hells Angels, England, explains:

[Our] gang was ordinary grease, or what most people called Rockers. I wasn't involved enough to be aware of the difference between our group and others, but I soon learned. The Mods were on one side. We, the Rockers, were on the other and no one else seemed to matter. The Mods were our automatic enemies and we were theirs. Why it came about, I don't know. It was the accepted system – our code of ethics, and we lived and breathed for it only.[30]

Being a South London rocker in the 1960s was an exciting business – at least, it seemed exciting at the time. Skiving off work to spend the day strutting around in groups, resplendent in studded-leather jackets, greasy jeans and cherry-red boots, life took on a whole new air of adventure. I still remember how I felt at the time. I ate, slept and dreamed motorbikes as before, only now I was something special. I was 'one of the boys', a rocker, and something to be reckoned with. We were definitely *the business*, and we made damn sure that everybody knew it. Not for us the dubiously effeminate world of the mods and their phony soul music, discos, mohair suits and pills. We didn't need artificial stimulants. We could get all the adrenalin rush we needed just by riding our bikes and blowing their 'hairdryers' into the weeds at the same time. All the papers said that we were past our peak and doomed to disappear. Boys were getting smarter, they said; cleaning up their act, they said; getting all the girls, they said. Well, screw them. We didn't give a fuck what the 'experts' thought. We knew better. We might be down but we certainly weren't out of the game.

Back came the Bank Holiday runs. Now there was a good reason for going away mob-handed

– there was a war to be won. You know, it's a funny thing, but I can't remember us ever actually hating the mods. We thought they were ridiculous, riding scooters decked out like Christmas trees, festooned with spotlights, mirrors and tigers' tails, wearing parkas, berets and *Ready Steady Go!* tee shirts. The whole thing was, quite plainly, laughable. But aside from a series of much publicized set-piece battles, advertised by the press, stage-managed by the police and resulting in only minor injuries, daily life was little more violent than before. Of course we were enemies, but we had to coexist in the real world without constant aggravation. After all, most of us had grown up together, lived on the same housing estates, gone to the same schools and slogged away on the same shop floors. In reality, it was the ritual that was all-important – to be seen to hate each other and thereby keep our respective images as hard men untarnished and our egos intact. The rockers hung out down at the local youth club; the mods got together in the Wimpy Bar. We knew where they were and they knew where we were, yet we very seldom interfered with each other unless it couldn't be avoided or unless either of us had got out of our heads and bravado overcame common sense. Away from the sea front and out of the public gaze, it was much more a war of words, a battle of insults, than a prolonged campaign to wipe each other off the face of the earth with fists and boots.

Reading through the newspaper reports of the period, the impression gained is very different indeed. The mass media had a field day with mods and rockers. It made for some really beautiful copy:

'Jail these wild ones – Call by MPs'
    Daily Mirror, 1 April 1964
'Goths by the sea'
    Evening Standard, 18 May 1964
'Marauding army of Vikings going through Europe massacring and plundering, living by slaughter and rapacity'
    The Star, Sheffield, 18 May 1964

'Mutated louts wreaking untold havoc on the land'

Time and Tide, 21 May 1964

'Magistrate orders youths to be cleansed'

The Times, 19 May 1965

'Make the rockers dig' and 'hard labour for mods'

Hastings and Thanet Gazette, April 1966

The press really got into the game, and played their part with all the enthusiasm they could muster. Murder, rape, pillage, drug taking – where would it all end? When would it be safe for Mum, Dad and Auntie Flo to go back on the beach? It seemed as though the very fabric of society was in imminent danger of collapse. Isn't it strange how the press can see things going on that are invisible to those actually involved? It makes you wonder ...

In its report on the latest round of beach football, the London Evening Standard of 18 June 1964 really went over the top and stated:

There are two kinds of youth in Britain today. There are those who are winning the admiration of the world by their courageous and disciplined service in the arduous mountain, jungle or desert territory – in Cyprus, on the Yemen border, in Borneo. And there are the Mods and Rockers, with their flick knives.

Seems like killing was an admirable thing for young men to indulge in, providing, of course, that it was all in a good cause and didn't take place in front of holidaymakers ...

In reality, of course, the mods' and rockers' conflict was spectacular but short-lived. By 1966 the whole thing was rapidly running out of steam. The coastal battles had largely disappeared as the respective combatants had become bored with it all. There was still trouble, and much publicized it was too, but the initial momentum had gone, and the action had become a mechanical farce. The game continued to be played, but the players had lost interest in the result. It was left to the gentlemen of the

press to wring every last drop of newsworthy blood from the corpse. Cohen sums up the position very well:

Like the last spurts of a craze or fashion style, the behaviour was often manifested with an exaggerated formalism. There was a conscious attempt to repeat what had been done two or three years before by actors who almost belonged to another generation. The media ... seized on to this behaviour, gave it new names and attempted to elevate it to the Mods and Rockers position. In places like Skegness, Blackpool and Great Yarmouth, the new hooligans were called by the press ... 'Greasers', 'Trogs' or 'Thunderbirds'. But such casting was not successful, even when there was an attempt to make the actors look even worse than the Mods and Rockers [as they, in turn] had been made to look worse than the Teddy Boys.[31]

Eventually, even the media, resourceful though it undoubtedly was, found itself unable to sustain public interest in mods and rockers and moved on to expose the evil doings of a new group of 'folk devils' – hippies – which had just arrived on our shores from America, threatening to debase public morality even further.

The conflict with the mods did, however, have an important and lasting impact on the bike scene. It attracted a new generation of kids to bikes, probably for all the wrong reasons. But once they'd got a taste for life on two wheels, the original motive behind the selection of that particular form of transport was forgotten, and they became firmly committed to the lifestyle.

Probably the most remarkable thing about the entire mods and rockers episode was that it conferred a stamp of legitimacy and permanency on the very group that all the social pundits predicted would rapidly run out of steam and disappear – the rockers. In fact, it was their opposite number – that bright new hope for youth, the mods – who could not stand the pace, who abandoned their principles along with their scooters and split up into a profusion of new media-created subcultures – soul boys, rude boys, suedeheads, skinheads, etc., etc. In its heyday the mod experience may indeed have been, as Pete Townshend suggested in a 1968 interview with *Rolling Stone* magazine, 'the closest thing to patriotism that I've ever felt', but even by 1965 the rot was beginning to set in:

there were [already] several strands within the Mods scene, and the more extravagant Mods – who were too involved in the whole rhythm and blues camp, Carnaby Street scene, to really 'need' the weekend clashes – began merging into the fashion-conscious hippies and their music began to grow closer to underground sounds. The others were never distinctive enough to maintain any generational continuity.[32]

So, when all's said and done, the mod phenomenon was no more than a phase, a fashion, a hype, which was wholly incapable of sustaining its initial impetus and cohesion. (How many scooters do you see on the road today?) Rockers, on the other hand, were possessed of a far greater tenacity. They had a history and, what's more, they had a future. Inevitably, changes had to be made in order to ensure survival, but nevertheless survive they did.

Meanwhile, on the other side of the Atlantic Ocean a potentially explosive mixture was bubbling. In the streets of San Francisco, the freaks of the bike world were resurfacing and consorting with the freaks of the middle class and coalescing within the alternative culture. The 'White Rabbit' was burning rubber along the highway, and 'Up against the wall, [any] motherfucker' who stood in his way. The old motorcycle subculture was dead. Long live the new . . .

FULL CIRCLE: THE WILD ONE IS REBORN IN HAIGHT-ASHBURY

He rides a road that don't have no end
An open highway without any bends
Tramp and his stallion alone in a dream
Proud in his colours as the chromium gleams

On Iron Horse he'll fly, on Iron Horse he'd gladly die
Iron Horse his wife, Iron Horse his life

He lives his life, he's livin' it fast
Don't try to hide when the dies have been cast
Riding a whirlwind that cuts to the bone
Wasted for ever, ferociously stoned

On Iron Horse he'll fly, on Iron Horse he'd gladly die
Iron Horse his wife, Iron Horse his life

One day, one day they'll go for the sun
Together they'll fly on the eternal run
Wasted for ever on speed, bikes and booze
Yeah, us and the brothers we're all born to lose

On Iron Horse he'll fly, on Iron Horse he'd gladly die
Iron Horse his wife, Iron Horse his life
Tramp and Lemmy, 'Iron Horse'

We are all outlaws in the eyes of Amerika . . .
Jefferson Airplane

Argggggghhhh – about 3 p.m. they started hearing it.

It was like a locomotive about ten miles away. It was the Hells Angels in 'running formation', coming over the mountain on Harley-Davidson 74s. The Angels were up there somewhere, weaving down the curves on Route 84, gearing down – thragggggghhhh – and winding up, and the locomotive sound got louder and louder until you couldn't hear yourself talk any more, or Bob Dylan rheumy and – thraaaaaaaaagggghhh – here they came round the last curve, the Hells Angels, with the bikes, the beards, the long hair, the sleeveless denim jackets with the death's head insignia and all the rest, looking their most royal rotten, and then one by one they came barrelling in over the wooden bridge up to the front of the house; skidding to a stop in explosions of dust, and it was like a movie or something – each one of the outlaws bouncing and gunning across the bridge with his arms spread out in a tough curve to the handlebars and then skidding to a stop, one after another after another.[33]

Date: Saturday 7 August 1965. Place: the La Honda ranch of writer and LSD innovator Ken Kesey, San Mateo County, California. Event: the first 'official' party held by the Merry Pranksters, the deviants of the American drug subculture, for the Hells Angels, the deviants of the motor-cycle subculture. This was the day the Angels became the toast of the intellectual-hip com-munity, the day the roughest and craziest of bikers were introduced to the twin delights of acid and free love. More important, it was the day that the outlaw bike culture ceased to be famous (or infamous) simply for smashing up bars in sleepy, hick towns and began instead to achieve a fresh notoriety as the shock troops of the counter-culture – the mechanized hippies who openly declared that love and peace were just a cop-out.

The Pranksters, in their desire to freak out even the freaks, had opened the door to the Angels and, almost overnight, the Angels' image was once again cool. It was as if the ghost of Marvin's Chino had at long last taken his revenge on Brando's Johnny, stomping him into the ground for good measure. As Tom Wolfe describes it, in his brilliant chronicle of events, *The Electric Kool-Aid Acid Test*:

The news spread around intellectual-hip circles in the San Francisco–Berkeley area like a legend . . . [The Pranksters] had broken through the worst hang-up that intellectuals know – the real-life hang-up. Intellectuals were always hung up with the feeling that they weren't coming to grips with real life. Real life belonged to all those funky spades and prize fighters and bullfighters and dock workers and grape pickers and wetbacks. Nostalgia de la boue. Well, the Hells Angels were real life. It didn't get any realer than that . . .[34]

The bikers, for their part, had no complaints. From being outcasts even among their fellow motorcyclists, they suddenly became sought-after personalities. They were courted by writers, religious mystics and political activists,

all anxious to discover their philosophy of life. They were invited to plush Hollywood parties and befriended by film stars and rock musicians. By some quirk of nature they had arrived, and their arrival was noted by working-class motor-cyclists and middle-class hippies alike.

Unlike the hippie, the outlaw biker was not prepared passively to accept the 'fun-loving' citizen's digs about his gender or inquiries about whether or not his mother was a baboon. He fronted out the citizen and said, 'If you don't like what you see – fuck off.' As Angela Carter writes:

Even the biker's clothing [is] 'the clothing of pure affront, sported to bug the squares . . . [and] always succeeds in bugging the squares no matter how often they are warned, "He only does it to annoy."'

The . . . Californian motorcycle gangs deck themselves with iron crosses, Nazi helmets, necklets and earrings, they grow their hair to their shoulders and dye their beards green, red and purple; they cultivate halitosis and body odour. Perfect dandies of beastliness, they incarnate the American nightmare. Better your sister marry a Negro than have the Oakland chapter of the Hells Angels drop in on her for coffee.[35]

And it was not just the Hells Angels. Outlaw motorcycle clubs throughout America, which had existed in a cultural vacuum since the mid-1950s, harassed by the police and cold-shouldered by the general public, now found themselves once again an object of interest. Kids just out of high school began to copy their style of dress, donning sleeveless denim jackets and shades, crudely imitating what they imagined to be their heroes' way of life. The mystique which surrounded the two-wheeled rebels of the Woodstock nation transcended class barriers. White American youth, from the Mexican border all the way to Canada and be-yond, took to the highways and byways in search of Paradise on beat-up motorcycles. Suddenly you no longer had to be interested in bikes to be a biker – it was the experience, not the nuts and bolts, that counted. Out there on the road, zapping open the throttle and feeling the surge of power hit you like a methedrine rush, you too could be Sonny Barger. Rebels, after all, didn't need a cause.

The bike became a kind of drug. Like acid, it assaulted the senses of the user, wrenching him both bodily and mentally from his earth-bound existence. As with acid, it was the trip that counted, not the destination. That was what the straights couldn't understand, what the authorities couldn't control. Only those who had shared that experience knew. Everybody else could go to hell.

Outlaws? They were outlaws by choice, from the word go, all the way out in Edge City. Further! The hip world, the vast majority of the acid heads, were still playing the eternal charade of the middle-class intellectuals – Behold my wings! Freedom! Flight! – but you don't actually expect me to jump off that cliff, do you? ... In their heart of hearts, the heads of Haight-Ashbury could never stretch their fantasy as far out as the Hells Angels. Overtly, publicly, they included them in – suddenly, they were the Raw Vital Proles of this thing, the favourite minority, replacing the spades. Privately, the heads remained true to their class, and to its visceral panics ...[36]

On Haight Street the bikers became the policemen of psychedelia. They protected and they prospered. The exploits of their leaders drifted into the folklore of the heads, who respected their upfrontedness and at the same time feared their wrath. It was a weird relationship but nevertheless one from which both groups profited. The bikers lived easily and well, and the heads were spared the worst excesses of the pushers and the police. When much respected Hells Angel leader Chocolate George lost his life in a bike smash on the way to the Fillmore, thousands of flower children flocked to his funeral and memorial party in San Francisco's Golden Gate Park. The Grateful Dead played free to the assembled mourners – bikers and hippies were united in their grief for a fallen comrade. Nicholas Von Hoffman, a writer and reseacher, recalls the event:

Henry J. Kaiser, 'the Bay Area tycoon', as the papers called him, and Chocolate George were buried on the same day. Chocolate George's funeral was more lively ...

The Berkeley Barb ran a drawing of Chocolate with a halo and a heart, looking like a canonized saint. In the article they said the dead Angel in his coffin looked like 'Attila the Hun. A fur cap hides his bare head, shaved when the doctors tried to repair the skull Chocolate broke when he flipped over the handlebars of his Harley.' It was a big affair in a number of Haight-Ashbury circles. Papa Al ... came and so did guys from half a dozen other bike clubs ... the Gypsy Jokers, the Cossacks, the Galloping Geese, and the LA Angels (all the way from LA).[37]

Even Charles Manson, the Devil himself, was anxious to include the bikers within his grand scheme of things, imagining that when Helter Skelter eventually came down they would rally to his cause and become his 'dune buggy army', the vanguard of the Family's apocalyptic crusade against the 'piggies'. Fortunately for all concerned, the bikers considered Charlie to be a bit of a joke. Apart from accepting the sexual favours offered by Manson's girls, they wanted nothing whatever to do with the whole business, much to the disappointment of the Los Angeles DA's office and the world's press, who were hungry to establish a connection between the two groups of 'undesirables'. Now that really would have made a story ...

CAPTAIN AMERICA AND THE BUCKSKIN KID

Get your motor running
Head out on the highway.
Looking for adventure
And whatever comes your way.
Yeah darling gonna make it happen
Take the world in a love embrace
Fire all the guns at once
And explode into space.
Like a true nature's child
We were born, born to be wild
Gonna fly so high, never gonna die.
Born to be wild
Born to be wild ...
    Steppenwolf, 'Born to be Wild'[38]

While the heads, bored by spannerwork, and shocked by Altamont, drifted on to different highs, the interest generated by the popularization of the biker lifestyle did not die. 'Born to be Wild' became the international anthem of a new generation of bikers. It was the release in 1969 of the film *Easy Rider* which, more than any other single event, projected the biker image beyond the self-constructed boundaries of the Californian outlaw clubs and the San Francisco heads. Rejected by Hollywood as uncommercial, the film was a box-office smash, capturing the hearts and minds of all who reached adolescence during the socially and politically turbulent 1960s. The decade had witnessed the release of a whole host of bike-related movies – *The Wild Angels*, *Born Losers*, *Hells Angels on Wheels*, *The Glory Stompers*, *Motor-Psycho* – to name but a few. They all plagiarized the same formula adopted so successfully by Stanley Kramer in *The Wild One* ten years before. But the world had moved on; it had all been done before, and done so much better, by Brando and Co.

Easy Rider cost a mere $375,000 to make. But it grossed more than $20 million for the distributors, Columbia Pictures. It was undoubtedly the road movie of the decade, if not of all time, portraying as it does, with a spine-chilling accuracy, the miasma of paranoid brutality that lurks uneasily behind the carefully groomed façade of the Land of the Free. 'Why should a film point out morality?' asked Peter Fonda, one of the film's stars. 'Kids don't like to be lied to while they're being preached at. The generation gap is less now than it was in my father's day. There's no respect if there's no communication...'[39]

Easy Rider opens with our two heroes – Wyatt, played by Peter Fonda in pre-Captain America guise, and his sidekick, Billy, played by Dennis Hopper – buzzing through the countryside on nondescript dirt-bikes. It soon becomes clear, however, that the two are not just trucking around having a good time but are really into something far more serious – maybe pulling off a major coke deal and making themselves a whole pile of money in the process. The mood of the film suddenly changes and a magically transformed Captain America and Billy 'head out on the highway' astride a pair of gleaming Harley choppers, to the music of

Steppenwolf's 'Born to be Wild'.

In an instant the new scene is set, and the viewer becomes increasingly aware that what he's watching is far from being just another biker movie. It transpires that their stash money is to be used to finance a run to the New Orleans Mardi Gras. Why? Who knows? We are told nothing of their past, their ideals, their aims or their aspirations. We don't know where it is they've come from; we've no option but to go along with the flow, to sink our egos into theirs and become part of the trip. The past no longer has any relevance. It has vanished. All that concerns us now is being in motion – 'looking for adventure and whatever comes our way'.

We travel with Captain America and Billy as they make their way across the heartland of the United States towards their appointed destination. Along the road they meet up with a number of different characters, all engaged, to some degree, in their own search for the meaning of life and all doomed to fall by the wayside as the travellers journey on. The Mexican family that feeds them, the members of the hippie commune who make love to them – each has its attractions, but there can be no stopping, no detour, no turning back.

Whatever lies in store for them they have to meet head-on. They drift into a small town and somehow get involved in a carnival parade, attracting the unwelcome attention of the sheriff's department. Thrown into jail, they encounter a whisky-drinking lawyer named George Hanson, played by Jack Nicholson. George too is an outcast in his own way and decides to go along with them in their quest.

The meeting with George is the key to the whole film. His rebellion is more concrete, more real, than that of the two bikers. He has a history, a purpose, a reason for hating the system, while they are nothing more than non-involved drifters, deliberately steering clear of anything that threatens to intrude upon their own narrow definition of freedom. George brings them down to earth; he makes them think about what they're doing and why they're doing it. And, predictably, as soon as they begin to think, the illusion is shattered and the dream turns into a nightmare.

Released from jail, the three of them take off together. George packs behind Fonda, looking incongruous beside the bikers in his white suit and gold baseball helmet, still clutching a bottle of bourbon. Pulling into a redneck café for a bite to eat, they are treated to a tirade of abuse from the clientele.

Later that night, after introducing George to the delights of smoking marijuana, they bed down around the camp fire and are attacked by townspeople armed with pick-axe handles. George is brutally clubbed to death, paying the ultimate price for his brief taste of life on the road.

In the process of exploring the American myth of freedom of the road, the two bikers discover that it is just that – a myth. George, their new friend, is touched, too, by the quest for this elusive freedom, but is ... cowardly murdered by mindless conformists, inflicted with the very same disease that killed the American myths of liberty and individuality – paranoia that stems from a fear of freedom.[40]

As George himself puts it: 'This used to be a helluva good country. There's a lot of talk about freedom and the individual, but no freedom. Show the people a little individualism and they're terrified...'[41]

MOVE OVER, MARLON, 'CAUSE THE BOYS ARE BACK IN TOWN

*This disc concerns those pouting prima donnas found within the
swelling J. Arthur ranks of the sexational psycle sluts. Those nubile
nihilists of the North Circular, the lean leonine leatherette lovelies of the
Leeds intersection, love to have her angels locked in the pagan paradise.
No cash, a passion for trash, the tough madonna whose crow magnon
face and crab nebular curves haunt the highway of the UK, whose harsh
credo captures the collective libido like lariats, their lips pushed in the
neon arc of dodgems. Delightfully disciplined, dumb but deluxe,
deliciously deranged. Twin-wheeled existentialists steeped in the sterile
excrement of a doomed democracy; whose post-Nietzchean sensibility
rejects the bovine gregariousness of a senile oligarchy; whose god is
below zero, whose hero is a dead boy condemned to drift like forgotten
sputniks in a fool's orbit, bound for a victim's future in the pleasure
dromes and ersatz bodega bars of the free world. The mechanicals of
love grind like organs of iron to a standstill; hands behind your backs in
the noxious gas of cheek to cheek totalitarianism. Hail the psycle sluts!
Go, go the Glan Gringos for the gonad age of cunnilingus! The dirty
thirty, the naughty forty, the shifty fifty, the filthy five. Zips, clips, whips
and chains wait for you to arrive. Hells Angels by the busload, stoned
stupid, how they strut, smoke Woodbines till they're banjoed and smirk
at the Swedish schmut, life on the straight and narrow path drives you
off your nut. By day you are a psychopath, by night you are a psycle
slut. On the BSA with two bald tyres, you drove a million miles. You cut
your hair with rusty pliers and you suffer with pillion piles, you get built
in obsolescence, travel in your guts, but you don't reach adolescence,
slow down you psycle sluts! Motorcycle Michael wants to buy a tank,
only 29 years old and he's learning how to wank. Yesterday he was in
the groove, today he is in a rut. My how the moments move, brute fun
psycle sluts. See cats on your originals, you peepee on his boots. He
makes love like a footballer: he dribbles before he shoots. The goings on
at the gang-bang ball made the citizens tut, tut, tut, but what do you
care, piss all, you tell 'em, psycle sluts. Boyfriend's burned his jacket,
ticket expired, tyres are knackered, knackers are tired. You can tell your
tale to the gutter press, get paid to peddle smut. Now you've ridden the
road of excess that leads to the psycle slut so you can dine and wine on
stuff that's bound to give you boils. Hot dogs direct from Crufts done in
the diesel oil or the burger joint around the bend where the meals are
fast and skimpy, for you that's how the world could end, not with a
bang, but a Wimpy.*

John Cooper Clarke

In Britain, as well as in America, 1968 represented a turning point for the bike scene in more ways than one. New and challenging possibilities for excitement arose outside the old familiar patterns of life. The age of the hippie had arrived with a vengeance, bringing in its wake a whole plethora of entertaining options. Hippies were, for the most part, quiet, passive and creative – on the face of it, quite unlike the louder, more aggressive bikers. But for the latter, struggling to keep going in an increasingly hostile environment, the hippie scene was heaven-sent. Dope smoking and Country Joe were more than acceptable replacements for light ale and rock 'n' roll. Drugs were socially rebellious and very pleasant into the bargain. Pleasant too were the new-found delights of 'free love'. Summer weekends were now spent at pop festivals instead of fighting on the beaches, and the phrase 'trips to the coast' suddenly took on an entirely new meaning. Almost parasitically, the embryonic bike scene of the late 1960s grew to maturity within the hippie subculture, sharing its drugs, its music, its festivals, its squats and its women. British bikers, like their American counterparts, became an integral part of the hippie way of life, while at the same time openly, and sometimes violently, abusing their ever-forgiving hosts. But this uneasy and unlikely coalition did contribute in a very material way to the well-being of both groups and wasn't entirely one-sided. The bikers defended their non-violent charges against the aggression of straight society, keeping the drug squad off the festival sites and ensuring that the semi-stoned children of the love generation didn't get ripped off by unscrupulous concert promoters or dope dealers. It was a contingent of bikers who banded together with French anarchists and tore down the fences at the first Isle of Wight festival, letting thousands of hippies in to watch the bands for free, much to the chagrin of the organizers, who were shown up as the straight business men that they really were rather than the champions of the alternative society that they liked to pretend to be. Mike Brake sums it up: 'The hippies have shown that it can be pleasant to drop out of the arduous job of attempting to steer a difficult, unrewarding society. But when that is done, you leave the driving to the Hell's Angels...'[42]

British Bikers formed themselves into loose-knit clubs, emulating their American precursors as best they could by sewing outlaw patches on to their sleeveless denims and drawing up codes of conduct. Things began to change rapidly. Old-time rockers were growing their hair, wearing beads amd eagerly exploring the mind-bending properties of psychedelic drugs. At the same time they enjoyed the freedom symbolized by a speeding motorcycle. Bikers had at last found their place in the revolution, their own model of action. They eagerly lapped up the stories fed to them by the press about the doings of outlaw bikers in the States. No matter what reality lay behind the media portrayal of this new breed of bikers, they were heroes, rebels *par excellence*. The more the newspapers highlighted and berated their exploits, the more kids rallied to the flag.

You could take your middle-class radicals, your Tariq Alis, your Jane Fondas, and stick them. They were no more real than Peter Pan or, for that matter, Karl Marx, and certainly of no more relevance. Working-class kids also wanted to put two fingers up at straight society, but trudging round the streets of London waving Vietcong flags or sitting-in at the LSE, certainly wasn't their idea of how to go about it. Even if they could understand the arguments, they found it impossible to relate to the people making them. Even in the teeth of the revolution, class was still a very formidable hurdle to overcome.

In spite of all the changes experienced by youth during the 'summer of love', by no means all the bikers aspired to becoming 1 per centers. The majority of them definitely weren't looking for a head-on clash with society; they weren't nihilists; they simply wanted to do their own thing and have a good time doing it. But they were stuck in a cultural vacuum, unable to reconcile the apparently polar opposites of roaring around on motorcycles while at the same time living the laid-back life. After all, the new breed of bikers was only the tip of the iceberg, and British motorcyclists in general hadn't moved on very far in outlook from the caff days of the late 1950s and early 1960s. If anything, since the demise of the mods there had been retrenchment, an attempt to recapture the past. Black leather, greasy DA haircuts and rock 'n' roll were far from dead and were still considered to be the style of the rebellious biker throughout most of the land. (Even today the media seem to be unable to mention any incident concerning bikers without resorting to the pejorative description 'leather-jacketed youths'.) What was needed was a new identity which the bike rider could adopt, an identity which fitted the new way of looking at the world. As in the States it was the release of *Easy Rider* in the autumn of 1969 that provided that identity and banished the coffee-bar cowboy into the Dark Ages for ever.

We had all seen the pre-release publicity that appeared in the press for months before the film actually arrived on these shores. We knew that it was all about bikes and drugs and, needless to say, we wanted to see it. But not for one single moment did we realize just what a significant and lasting impact it would have on the British bike scene. It hit us like a bolt between the eyes – hardly twelve months had gone by since the first screening of what we had all come to regard as the greatest film of all time, *The Wild One*, and now suddenly all that belonged to the past. The release of *Easy Rider* transformed our idea, virtually overnight, of what was and what was not meant by the term 'biker lifestyle'. I first saw the film (I must have seen it at least a dozen times since) one dreary December evening at the Odeon, Leicester Square. I'd gone up to London on the train with a couple of mates because my bike was broken down, as usual. As we queued for our tickets the only thought in our minds was whether we would be rewarded by sufficient doses of sex, violence and drug abuse to justify the travelling and the quite severe financial outlay on luxu-

rious, red velvet seats that tilted back when you sat in them. It was a pretty peculiar setting in which to watch the tale of sin and savagery that I was expecting. But as the initial smash-bang image of Steppenwolf's 'Born to be Wild' dissolved into Captain America's and Billy's hauntingly surreal search for, or perhaps escape from, the American dream, we were already well and truly hooked. For me the film would have been a success without any plot or dialogue whatsoever. Just to watch the pair of them gunning their Harley across the screen with the wind in their hair, was poetry in itself. Incredible bikes, incredible music, incredible scenery – these were more than enough to impress me beyond words. Thinking back, it occurs to me that the depth of the sensations experienced probably owed a lot to the dope that we smoked, in copious quantities, throughout the performance. But, whatever the reason, *Easy Rider* was for us a truly messianic film that quite literally triggered off a thousand ideas in our eager, if slightly stoned, minds. It was like drifting off into another world, a world which we desperately wished to experience for ourselves. In that single ninety-four minute, budget movie, Dennis Hopper managed to encapsulate brilliantly the very spirit of freedom that we had all felt, at one time or another, out there on the road. He presented on the screen a ceremonial vindication of what we'd known all along but were unable to articulate. Even the numbing shock of the ending, the pointless death, was itself strangely beautiful. It said it all. There could have been no way more fitting, no other way that could have hammered home the message more effectively. Outlaws no longer had to be swaggering, macho bullies to offer a challenge to the world. All they had to do was place themselves beyond the comprehension of 'ordinary' people in order to qualify for summary extermination. They might be dead and gone, but the challenge had been made, and we were more than ready to take it up. We didn't talk very much as we made our way home on the last train from Charing Cross. We didn't need to. We understood.

Easy Rider gripped our world by the neck and shook it around. Nothing was ever the same again. It provided a clarity of image, a style which had hitherto been lacking, and it banished everything that had gone before into total obscurity. Black-leather jackets and quiffs weren't merely *passé*, they had become a sick joke. Now to cut any ice at all you just had to have that West Coast style – long hair, fringed suede jacket and shades *à la* Dennis Hopper. Looking cool was all-important. Even riding styles altered to conform with the new image. Doing the ton down the bypass, chin on the petrol tank, arse in the air, suddenly lost all its appeal. Now we rode our bikes along the high street, feet up and laid back inviting the citizens to turn their heads and comment as we passed by – in response to which we would remain unmoved, impassive, staring stonily ahead, seemingly oblivious of all the attention – looking cool. Bikers ceased trying to emulate TT racers and instead became street heroes in their own right. Even the vocabulary changed. Bikes became known as 'choppers', 'hogs' or simply 'wheels'. Birds became 'chicks' or 'old ladies'. Fights became 'rumbles' or 'stompings'. It was our very own revolution. The new bike scene was still alive and kicking, only now it wore a new set of clothes, spoke a new language and found new ways to outrage the public.

LOOKING BACK - STILL CRAZY AFTER ALL THESE YEARS

*Where there is a wanderlust spirit in the hearts of all bikers I shall
flourish in it . . .*

*Where there is an essence of brotherhood in a biker's lifestyle my heart
shall blend with it . . .*

*While there's one chained biker within prison walls I shall never be
rested or free . . .*

*While the bikers' legacy is ours to protect, Our lifestyle signifies the spirit
of our brotherhood.*

Crazy Horse Coppola, Vagos MC

More than thirty years have gone by since Brando's *The Wild One* spread the bikers' gospel beyond the highways of Southern California and out across the world. During those thirty years the biker nation has gone from strength to strength, becoming a truly international brotherhood. In the process it has established itself, without doubt, as the most pervasive and long-lived of all post-war subcultures. It has had its ups and downs, its twists and turns, and in some ways it has changed beyond all recognition since the first outlaw bikers hit the streets. Nevertheless, there exists a continuous thread which binds the modern-day biker to those who pioneered the lifestyle back in the 1940s. That thread is our legacy, our culture, our history, and we defend it with a fierce pride.

Today the tribes of the biker nation can be found in countries as diverse as New Zealand and Mexico, Austria and Brazil. We may not share a common language, but we do share a common belief – a belief in freedom and in brotherhood. We have a saying that goes like this: 'When we do right no one remembers, when we do wrong no one forgets . . .' We don't ask for charity, but we do ask for respect.

True outlaw bikers aren't the wild-eyed kids that the press is so fond of quoting. We may not be the most well-mannered or presentable people in the world, but we are probably the most honest. We have nothing to hide. We don't hand out bullshit, and we don't take bullshit. Our way of life isn't to everybody's taste, but neither is theirs to ours. Governments do their best to control us, to make us conform to their pattern of civilized behaviour. In the United States federal racketeering laws are abused to imprison our leaders. In West Germany our clubs are banned. In Canada Project Focus records our every movement. We get pilloried by the press, which prints lies about us, and by the police, who go out of their way to stop and hassle us. We are made to wear helmets to protect ourselves against lunatic car drivers. We get no support from 'concerned' MPs or civil rights organizations. But I guess we wouldn't have it any other way. We have our own voice; we fight our own battles; we choose our own friends; and we look after ourselves. We are the biker nation, and while we live and breathe we will protect our heritage. In the words of Hells Angel Sonny Barger: 'It's something we believe in. I know they can lock me up, and I know they can beat me up and I know they can kill me, but they're not going to change my mind. They're the assholes and I know it. They're mad because I know it.'[43]
Ride on, brother . . .

REFERENCES

1 The *Western Mail*, 1980.
2 F.J. Hobsbawm, *Bandits*, Harmondsworth, Penguin, 1972, p. 132.
3 H.R. Kaye, *A Place in Hell*, London, New English Library, 1970, pp. 7–8.
4 Ibid., p. 18.
5 Hunter S. Thompson, *Hells Angels*, Harmondsworth, Penguin, 1967, p. 75.
6 Kaye, *A Place in Hell*, pp. 13–14.
7 *Life* Magazine, 21 July 1947.
8 *Life* Magazine, 28 July 1947.
9 *Life* Magazine, 28 July 1947.
10 Thompson, *Hells Angels*, p. 76.
11 Jan Hudson, *The Sex and Savagery of Hells Angels*, London, New English Library, 1967, p. 14.
12 Ibid., p. 17.
13 Ibid., pp. 19–21.
14 George Wethern and Vincent Colnett, *A Wayward Angel*, London, Corgi, 1979, pp. 48–9.
16 Kaye, *A Place in Hell*, p. 39.
17 Donald Spoto, *Stanley Kramer, Film Maker*, New York, G.P. Putman, 1941, p. 157.
18 *Life* Magazine, 19 July 1972.
19 Spoto, *Stanley Kramer, Film Maker*, pp. 157–60 (quoting Stanley Kramer).
20 Thierry Sagnier, *Bike! Motorcycles and the People Who Ride Them*, New York, Harper & Row, 1974, pp. 22–3.
21 Gillian Freeman, *The Leather Boys*, London, New English Library, 1969, pp. 16–17.
22 Stuart Hall and Tony Jefferson (eds.), *Resistance through Rituals: Youth Subcultures in Post-War Britain*, London, Hutchinson, 1976, p. 81.
23 Ibid., pp. 60–1.
24 'At the Ball Tonight'.
25 T.R. Fyvel, *The Insecure Offenders*, Harmondsworth, Penguin, 1963, p. 55.
26 Ibid., pp. 60–1.
27 Stanley Cohen, *Folk Devils and Moral Panics*, London, Paladin, 1973, p. 192.
28 Jeff Nuttall, *Bomb Culture*, London, Paladin, 1970, pp. 32–3.
29 Cohen, *Folk Devils and Moral Panics*, p. 190.
30 Jamie Mandelkau, *Buttons: The Making of a President*, London, Sphere, 1971, p. 21.
31 Cohen, *Folk Devils and Moral Panics*, p. 200.
32 Ibid., p. 201.
33 Tom Wolfe, *The Electric Kool-Aid Acid Test*, London, Bantam, 1969, pp. 153–4.
34 Ibid., p. 158.
35 Angela Carter, 'Notes for a Theory of Sixties Style', *New Society*, 14 December 1967, p. 867.
36 Wolfe, *The Electric Kool-Aid Acid Test*, p. 326.
37 Nicholas Von Hoffman, *We Are the People Our Parents Warned Us Against*, Fawcett Premier, 1968, pp. 156–7.
38 *Easy Rider*, soundtrack, 1969.
39 Peter Fonda, quoted in Joe Morella and Edward Z. Epstein, *Rebels – The Rebel Hero in Films*, Secaucus, New Jersey, Citadel, 1973, p. 184.
40 Tex Campbell, 'Sixty-Nining at the Movies', *Easyriders Magazine*, No. 69.
41 *Easy Rider*, soundtrack.
42 Mike Brake, *The Sociology of Youth Culture and Youth Subcultures*, London, Routledge & Kegan Paul, 1980, p. 103.
43 Sonny Barger, in *F.T.W. Magazine*, 19 November 1980.

INDEX